TOO HOSTILE

NICOLE DYKES

FLETCHER

Man, it's a nice day. All sunny and warm, but not too hot. I could stay outside for the rest of the afternoon, but I have a class in about an hour, so it's really only enough time to grab something to eat, and then, it's back to campus.

But when I unlock my apartment door and push it open, I'm instantly greeted by a bombshell blonde with a huge smile on her face. She's clearly not bothered at all that she used her key to break into my place.

"Blair."

She walks right up to me, a brown bag and what looks like a coffee in her hands as she leans in and kisses my cheek. "You know, someday I'll get you guys to call me mom."

I grin at that. She's for sure the closest thing I've ever had to a mother. She's that for Rhett and Bree too—my adopted siblings. We all grew up together in foster care. We saw horrors no kids ever should, and then there was Blair. She and her now-husband, Rhys, scooped us up out of the abyss, and I haven't looked back since.

Okay—that's a lie. A total fucking lie, but it's one I tell myself, and that's what I'm sticking to.

"So *Mom*," I go over-the-top with the title, and she just shakes her head at me. "What brings you to my apartment today for a little breaking and entering?"

She shoves me slightly, though my sturdy frame doesn't budge, then hands me the bag and coffee. "Well, since you never call your mother, I thought I'd stop by to make sure you weren't dead."

I chuckle at that and open the bag, the smell of my all-time favorite meatball sub hitting my nostrils. "Fuck yes. You went to Mickey's just for me?"

She winks, grabbing her own coffee from my kitchen counter and taking a spot at one of the bar stools at the counter. "I did."

"You're my favorite mother ever," I tease as I take a seat by her. This apartment really isn't your typical college student's place. My parents don't hold back when it comes to their kids—at least the ones who'll let themselves be spoiled.

Rhett was never having that shit. Fought Blair and Rhys tooth and nail every time they wanted to buy him something. I guess I'm different. Blair is a caretaker, and if she wants to spoil me a bit here and there, who the hell am I to stop her?

She wants me to relax and enjoy college, so that's what I'm doing—in my extremely nice, two-bedroom apartment with wood floors and marble countertops. I swear this place is almost as nice as the house I've been lucky enough to call home with Rhys, Blair, Rhett, and Bree.

I smile, thinking about how much that house freaked us all out at first. It's huge. They have a heated outdoor pool, indoor gym, and tons of bedrooms. None of us had ever seen a place so big, so nice, or so clean before.

We all tiptoed around there for what felt like forever before Blair made it very clear that it was our home and she wasn't going to freak out if we broke something or made a mess. She proved her point by throwing a glob of spaghetti at Rhys when we were eating dinner one night.

We were all scared shitless that the large, stoic man would fly off the handle, but he only smirked and tossed some right back at her. Not caring that she was wearing an expensive white blouse.

She then hit Rhett right in the face, and when Bree, Rhett, and I looked at each other, it was like we could finally breathe again. And then it was on. I smile at the memory, and Blair doesn't miss it. "What has you smiling?"

"Just thinking about the spaghetti food fight."

"Ah yes. When you kids finally started trusting me a little bit." She's smiling big, and she has a lightness to her tone, but I know she's not totally unaffected. Man, we were hard on her.

We didn't mean to be. But when you grow up the way we did, it's kind of hard to let people in. All we ever had was each other, and then, here comes Blair and Rhys, loving us for absolutely no reason.

"And then you go and break into my place," I joke. Not only does she pay for this place—she's welcome, no matter what, even if she didn't. But she doesn't point out that she's paying for my whole damn life at the moment.

Nope. Blair isn't like that.

"I missed you," she says as I tear into my sandwich, which has her sighing and grabbing napkins to thrust at me. I take them and wipe at my mouth, even though I'm still busy devouring my food. "Missed you too."

She lets me eat as she sips at her coffee, and when I'm finished, I let out a loud belch and pat my very full stomach.

"Damn, that was good."

"You, my dear son, are a slob," she says, using a spare napkin to wipe at my chin.

"Thanks for lunch, but is everything really okay? Max and Ian?"

She's smiling big, so that's a good sign. Max and Ian only moved in with them a little while ago. They're foster kids like us. Rhett and Grayson, Rhett's boyfriend, met them while volunteering at the city mission downtown. Max wound up in the hospital because of a drunk abusive motherfucker, and the very thought of it sends chills down my spine.

Thoughts of the past come bubbling up, and I have to stand up from the stool and gather my trash, hoping for a distraction.

"They're fine, sweetie." Blair misses nothing. Her hand moves to my wrist, covering it and stopping my hand from shaking.

3

Max and Ian are safe.

I have to remind myself of that. They're living with Blair, Rhys, and Bree now. They're safe. No one is ever going to hurt them again.

"Deep breaths, honey." Goddammit. I almost hate that she knows me so well. She's standing now, and her hands are on both sides of my face as I struggle to control my rapid breathing. I get control of myself and take in a shaky breath as I look into her eyes.

How does this still happen? Why the hell can't I just move on already?

"Max and Ian are doing well," she says calmly. "Really well. They even like school, and Max has been drawing nonstop." When she smiles, I smile too and then nod my head.

"Good. That's good."

"Nothing is wrong," she says, and I take another deep breath and release it. "Everything is okay. I just missed you."

I force another smile. "I just saw you last week."

"Doesn't mean I didn't miss you, you little shit." she teases, and finally, it's like I come back to myself and am able to actually smile.

"I missed you too."

She releases me and grabs her coffee again, taking a drink. "Good. Anyway I just wanted to make sure you were eating. May have had some groceries delivered and stocked your fridge a bit."

I shake my head at her because she's never stopped taking care of me or my brother and sister since the day she took us in. "Thank you," I say simply, not really wanting to get mushy but so damn grateful all the same.

"When is class?" I'm honestly surprised she doesn't have my schedule memorized, although knowing her, she probably does.

"I have to get going pretty soon. Professor Barlowe hates when I'm late." Which I have been all too often—maybe because I really like it when he gets all growly. Why? Don't ask me. I haven't spent too long examining that, but man, do I love irritating that man.

"So I'm sure you do your best to be on time often then." She gives me a knowing smile.

"Yup. Can't imagine why the guy doesn't like me."

4

She frowns at that, squishing my cheeks her finger and thumb. "It's impossible not to like you, sweetie."

"You might be a bit biased there, Blair."

She tosses her head back and cackles happily at that. "Walk me out to my car, kiddo. I suppose I'll leave you to it."

I smile at that and walk her out of my apartment, taking the time to lock the door, even though I'm not really sure why. My own mom breaks into my place. My smile is comfortable as I walk with her down to her car. She unlocks it but doesn't open the door yet. "Bree is graduating soon."

I give her a quick nod, not missing the proud yet sad smile on her face. "Yeah, I know."

Bree is my age, but I graduated from high school a year before I was supposed to, along with Rhett's class. "You'll be there?"

I nod. It was already in my plans. "Wouldn't miss it."

She's smiling brightly now. "Good. Grayson and Rhett will be there too, along with a lot of guys from the tattoo shop." I nod along as she lists people off because I have no doubt Blair is going all out for Bree's graduation party, despite my sister likely hating that idea.

But Blair means well. "I'll be there."

She leans in and kisses my cheek. "Good. Now get to class, so you don't upset your professor." She pulls her door open and then gives me a mischievous grin. "Speaking of professors . . ." She waggles her eyebrows at me, "Any hotties?"

I nearly choke on my own spit in surprise—why I'm surprised at this point with Blair, I'm really not sure. The woman never holds back. "What? No."

"Oh, come on. Don't tell me you don't have a thing for a hot older professor. I totally get it. And back in college—"

"Mom," I say exaggeratedly, my hand dragging over my face. "I'm begging you not to finish that sentence."

She chuckles, "Oh, you know it's only Rhys for me now. Doesn't mean I didn't have a life before that. A naughty one." She waggles her eyebrows at me, and I fake gag.

"Please stop," I beg.

She rolls her eyes at me and tosses her hands, like I'm the crazy one. "Fine. I won't go there, but there's nothing wrong with a little professor/college student lovin'."

I stare at her and then shake my head, laughing. "Pretty sure it's against school rules, and I'm also pretty sure you aren't supposed to encourage that as a parent."

She waves me off easily. "You're an adult, Fletcher. Live a lot."

I can't help laughing, still shaking my head at the best woman I've ever known. God, do I love her. "The saying is live a *little*."

"Eh, life is short. Live a lot. Love a lot." She brushes her hand over my cheek, and I lean into it just a little. "But be safe. Condoms and all that stuff." She winks, and I shake my head yet again and sigh.

"Bye, Blair."

"Bye sweetie." She blows me a kiss as she climbs into her car and shuts the door. I wave to her, and after she leaves, I start the short walk to campus. I can't help but think on the way to my Economics class about the conversation with Blair.

Why the hell didn't I admit that maybe I do have a little bit of a crush on a professor? It's not like Blair isn't cool with it—hell, way too damn cool with it, in fact.

But as I walk along the sidewalk on campus, taking in the freshly cut green grass, I know why I didn't fess up to it. Because when Blair was talking about a hot professor, no doubt, she was assuming there was a bossy, strong female type who caught my eye. Which would be my type.

In fact, I have one female professor who fits that description to a T, but it isn't her who's invaded my dreams—both at night and during the day. No, Professor Crawford is fine, even a little flirty, but she's not on my mind.

She doesn't get my blood flowing and my mind stuck on lengthy dirty fantasies.

The professor I can't stop thinking about has dark, short hair that's perfectly tousled, like he spends far too much time running his fingers through it when he's frustrated—which is a lot, if my time around him is any indication.

He's always wearing a suit or dress shirt and pants, all buttoned-up and serious, making me wonder what's underneath those stuffy clothes. I know it's a hard, muscular body. There's no doubt in my mind he's firm and solid, perfectly sculpted. I've wasted countless hours picturing just what he looks like naked.

Does he have hair covering his body? Or is he mostly bare? Is he defined with no fat at all, or does he have some cushioning? Honestly, I wouldn't care either way, for the record. My instincts tell me it's the former. I haven't seen a hint of extra weight on the man.

But he's a mystery, that's for damn sure.

He wears a little bit of scruff most of the time, neatly trimmed, but you couldn't really call it a beard. His eyes are a dark hazel that burn into my soul as he lectures me for being too loud and tardy all too often.

His lips are a soft, pale pink that look so soft, it makes my mouth water, thinking about getting a taste. Just one. I'd give anything for that moment of bliss I know it would be.

Professor Ronan Barlowe letting his guard down and giving in just for a moment.

What would that be like?

Heaven. That's all I can imagine it would be. Then hell, when he'd undoubtably push me away. Because one thing I know from an entire semester of being obsessed with the man is he doesn't let his guard down—not ever.

And though Blair would have been totally cool with it, all of it, if I'd have told her, I just couldn't.

Because everyone thinks I'm straight.

When I'm really, really . . . not.

RONAN

He's late again. *This little shit.* I swear to God, I'm only twenty-six years old, and he's going to give me a stroke. An actual goddamn stroke from the anger flowing through my veins when he saunters into my classroom with that cocky damn smile on his way too handsome face.

No. Not handsome. He's a kid. A damn spoiled brat. A real pain in my ass. Good-looking or not, it doesn't matter to me in the slightest.

"Late again, Mr. Moore?" I try to sound bored, but I know he hears my irritation. I can't hide it when it comes to Fletcher Moore. He gets under my skin. He makes my blood boil with his nonchalant, careless attitude.

Not a care in the world, this one.

I have no doubt he's had everything handed to him. He's never had to worry about a damn thing in his life, and he has no problem walking in here three minutes after the bell.

He just flops into a chair in the front row and shrugs. "Really couldn't be helped today, Professor." I hate the way he says *Professor*. It rolls off his tongue far too easily. Almost like a purr, his eyes flashing with a sinister, menacing delight.

"No?" I ask, keeping my voice even and calm, even though I want to challenge him. I want to make him see how arrogant and annoying he really is.

"Nope." The *p* in the word pops on his full lips, a smirk forming right after. "My mom broke into my place."

There are snickers all around the packed lecture hall, and I can feel the vein in my neck throbbing.

Yup. This is how I die. I'm going to stroke out right here in what used to be my happy place. Teaching economics may seem like a boring path to me, but I love it. I've loved every second of being a college professor, except when cocky assholes like Fletcher Moore walk in here like they own the place.

I'm in charge here.

Not. Him.

And so far, he's been the absolute worst. Completely and totally unconcerned.

"And how exactly did your mother do that?" I ask, although I'm not sure why I bother. I should just go on with the lecture. Mr. Moore has stolen more than enough time from my class today.

But I swear everyone in the room is waiting with bated breath for the all too charming young man—little shithead— to answer my question. "Well, she has a key." He shrugs his oversized shoulders again. He may act like a kid, and he may be a freshman in college, but the guy is built like a professional linebacker. Huge and muscled. Doesn't even try to hide it by wearing a blue and white tank top and shorts that hug his broad thighs. Nope.

I don't notice the way his arm muscles flex as he leans back in his chair confidently.

Nope. Not. At. All.

"Why does your mom have a key? You're nineteen." I'm assuming.

"Eighteen," he says with a smile, and I groan. It's the end of the year, most freshmen are nineteen, but he must have a summer birthday. "Just turned eighteen in January actually," he says far too proudly, and my eyes narrow at him.

"You started college before you turned eighteen?"

9

"Yup." Again, with that damn popping *p*. "Graduated from high school a year early."

My lips part in surprise, but I fight asking him anything about that. I also fight trying to wrap my head around that. He must have had that handed to him too. Maybe he was such a pain in the ass in high school, they just pushed him through.

That would make sense to me, for damn sure.

"You're still an adult." Although that word doesn't sound right to describe the guy. He's as childish as they come. Carefree. Unbothered. Annoying as fuck. "Why does your mother have a key to your place?"

And why the hell do I keep engaging with him? I have to stop.

His bicep flexes when he reaches behind his head to grasp the back of the chair, showing off trimmed dark hair under his pits and a thick vein that runs up the taut muscle.

I inadvertently lick my lips, then force my gaze away from his flexed arm.

Jesus fucking Christ. What if someone saw that?

I'm so damn glad this semester is almost over. Fletcher isn't going to be an economics major, no way in hell. So he's almost out of my damn hair and not my problem.

Two more weeks.

That's it.

"Well, she does pay for the place," he says effortlessly, like it's no big deal that he mooches off his parents.

"Your mother pays your rent?"

I hear more snickering all around us, but my eyes remain only on Fletcher. "Of course. You look annoyed, Professor." He smirks widely at me, and I feel my entire body tense up even more. "Shouldn't you love that? It's very economical."

My eyes nearly pop out of my head. The nerve of this kid. "You could get a job."

He just grins even more at me now, knowing without a doubt he's annoying the shit out of me. And likely knowing that I can't say shit to him because I don't want to lose my job. "Now, that doesn't sound very fun, Professor."

Yup. I'm not going to make it. There's no way. One of us is going to die this semester.

Two more weeks.

I grit my teeth. "Let's move on."

There are more pleased laughs from his classmates, and he just settles into his seat, clearly happy with himself, as I continue on with the lecture he so rudely interrupted. I'm not going to make it.

"I'M TELLING YOU, I'm not going to make it. This kid is the most arrogant little shithead I've ever seen." I toss back another gulp of my beer, and my best friend, Nathan, just groans loudly.

"Not this again."

"What?" I ask, turning to look at his irritated grimace.

"I cannot listen to you whine about Fletcher Moore another night. It's Friday night. I just want to drink a beer in my favorite bar and maybe play a game of pool without hearing about the infamous Fletcher Moore."

"No." Annie, our other friend and a professor at the college, just like Nathan and me, groans as she plops down on the bar stool next to Nathan. "I'm not doing it." She gestures for the bartender. "Gin and tonic, please, and make it strong."

The bartender grins and gives her a nod as she places her purse on the bar and looks past Nathan and right at me. "We aren't doing this again, are we?"

"Do what?" I ask grumpily. I swear these two are being very dramatic right now.

"You know what." Annie deadpans and gladly takes the drink the bartender places in front of her, taking a sip.

"I don't talk about him that much," I grumble and sift through the bowl of pretzels on the bar, picking one up and bringing it to my lips.

"You do," Nathan says very clearly, his eyes on mine and the irritation clear.

"He's a pain in the ass," I say. Nathan just shakes his head as I continue, "I mean, the kid is proud that his parents pay his way through everything. His mother pays his rent, and he considers that to be economical."

Annie shrugs and takes another sip of her drink. "I mean, he's not wrong."

I glance at my friend with no smile on my face because she can't be serious. "Really?"

She waves me off easily. We've known each other long enough, so I don't bristle because she's put up with me from day one. Literally. My first day on campus, I was a mess and totally lost, and there was Annie, showing me the way. She's about ten years older than me and knew her way around already.

She introduced me to Nathan that night at this very bar, and the rest is history. I don't trust many people, but these two and their spouses, I do.

"Listen, I know. We don't really need to go into the whole *Ronan Barlowe's sad little life* thing, do we?" She grins, and I can't help but laugh a little.

"Fuck you too."

She cackles and takes a drink of her gin and tonic. "I mean, I am a sociology professor, so don't get me wrong, I do love the whole sad backstory . . ."

"Again." I raise my middle finger at her. "Fuck. You." Normally, I'd be a little more refined, but it's Friday, and this bar is far enough from campus, I feel safe letting loose a little. It's one of the many reasons I like coming here.

She laughs, and Nathan grips my shoulder happily. They know my past. I've told them both pretty much everything. Something else I really don't do—and yes, it may have first come out because I had a little bit too much to drink—but it actually feels good to have someone else in the world know.

"I'm just saying, just because you had to literally work your way up from the bottom doesn't make his life any less valid."

I bristle. I'd like to think I don't judge people who appear to have had it easy, but then again . . . shit. Maybe I do a little. Not one thing was ever given to me, so maybe I am a little bitter.

"Besides, the kid is a genius."

I snort at that and take a drink, shaking my head. "No. He's not."

Annie doesn't back down, "No really. Like an actual genius. He hardly ever makes it to my class, and the kid aces every single test."

"Being lazy isn't equal to being a genius. Maybe he cheats on his tests," I offer.

Nathan just dismisses me, waving his hand. "She checked."

Annie laughs at that and nods. "I did. I had to. But ask Nathan here. Not one missed question on any algebra test."

Nathan shakes his head. "Nope. And that little asshole never shows up to the actual lectures. Although he is there for the smaller classes, and trust me, he isn't cheating."

"We've compared notes."

I'm suddenly annoyed I chose to teach at the small private college now because we all frequently have the same freshmen students in our intro classes. "He's not a genius. Maybe you both aren't watching closely enough."

The fact that he's actually a year younger than most freshmen sits in the back of my brain, but I push it away.

"I don't know," Nathan says, popping a pretzel into his mouth. "I see him in the library a lot."

"So?" I ask, hating that they seem to have a positive view of him when I'm just not willing to see that. He's an entitled little prick, and that's all there is to it.

"So, he's actually reading. Not like textbooks, but *reading*, reading. The kid is smart," Nathan says, and Annie agrees, nodding her head as he speaks.

I just huff like a child because I refuse to believe he reads for fun.

Fortunately, they move on quickly. Nathan pipes up excitedly, "Oh, did you hear about Professor Tuttle?"

"Rhonda?" I ask, and he nods.

"Yup."

"No," I answer absently. I don't know her well, but I can't imagine the gossip is that juicy. The woman is boring as hell. You think I'm buttoned-up and disciplined, you should see the late-thirty something.

"What happened?" Annie bites.

"Apparently, she was put on leave. Had an affair with a student that went south."

I nearly choke on a pretzel that gets lodged in my throat because I did not see that coming.

"What? Rhonda Tuttle was fucking a student?"

He nods, and Annie gasps, saying what I'm thinking, "No. Way."

"Yes way," Nathan confirms. "Apparently, she tried to break it off, but the kid went a little crazy. Wouldn't take the rejection."

"Jesus," I say incredulously. "She's married."

"She is," he confirms sadly. "It's going to be all over the news though, no doubt. She had to get a restraining order, and the kid has been all over social media. Claiming she seduced him and then just dumped him."

"That's brutal," Annie says, and I have to agree.

"Who the hell would want to sleep with a twenty-year-old?" I blurt because I can't imagine wanting to sleep with a student.

I mean, even if they don't look twenty. Built like a fucking house and gorgeous as all hell . . .

No. Absolutely not.

Even if I was attracted to someone who looks like Fletcher, which I'm absolutely not, if he acted like Fletcher, it would be nothing but a turnoff. I tend to go for older men. Mature. Can rent a fucking car and don't have to have their parents pay their rent.

"Yeah. I for sure don't get that. I didn't want to sleep with a twenty-year-old even when I was twenty," Annie says, and I grin.

"Careful, Ronan here is only twenty-six." Nathan wraps an arm around my shoulder and teases.

"Oh my God, I forgot you're a damn fetus," Annie jokes.

I shove Nathan off me playfully. "I'm not a fetus. I'm nothing like the freshmen we teach."

"True. No one would ever describe you as young and fun," Annie says, wiggling her eyebrows at me, and I roll my eyes at her with a familiar smile on my face because I can't seem to help it.

Most of the time, I hide my smile. I keep it completely professional when I'm on campus. I can't imagine throwing away my career and reputation for some likely inexperienced sex with a twenty-year-old who became clingy.

Because, of fucking course, he became clingy. She should have known better. His brain is still forming, for Christ's sake. "I can't believe she did that."

"I can't either," Nathan agrees. "She's not speaking, and neither is the college, but it's all over the news. It's a damn mess."

"Her ass is getting fired," Annie says nonchalantly as she eats a pretzel.

"As she should," I say because the rules are pretty damn clear. Why a professor would want anything to do with a student is beyond me. But anyone in a position of power should avoid a relationship with someone who's relying on them.

A cold chill goes through me as I think back to my early teen years. Of the feeling of being helpless and never being able to rely on one single soul.

A darkness settles over me, begging me to push it away. I don't want to go back there.

"Good riddance."

They both nod in agreement, and we move on to lighter topics as I do the all too familiar dance of forcing away the memories of my past and trying to convince my brain that I'm now safe.

A battle I'm not sure I'll ever actually win.

FLETCHER

"What can I do for you, Mr. Moore?" Goddamn, I love how growly his voice gets when he's irritated. Which around me, is 90 percent of the time.

I offer him my biggest, most charming smile—hell, I think I even bat my eyelashes at the man. When it comes to Professor Ronan Barlowe, I have no shame. Class just ended, and people are filing out, so I keep my voice fairly low. "I was wondering if you need a TA for next semester."

The man before me looks at me incredulously. And just stares for what feels like forever. I mean, honestly, I'm not one to get nervous, but the guy is making even me a little twitchy. "Are you serious?" He also keeps his voice pretty low but deadly as he looks me square in the eyes.

The last person leaves, but the door is open, and the halls are bustling. "Of course. Why not? I'm an excellent assistant," I say with a little hint of a tease to it.

Those hazel eyes are shooting downright daggers at me now. He looks almost murderous. And fuck, if that doesn't make my cock hard. I can't explain it. There's just something about this man that makes all common sense go out the window.

I know he's dangerous. I know he's a professor at the college I attend and that it's maybe a little inappropriate for me to have this big of an obsession with him. But the dude haunts my dreams. *What can I say?*

"No," he says firmly and simply before grabbing his bag and draping it across his chest, the strap lying over his broad shoulder.

He moves past me, but of course, I keep up with him, not able to let it go. "No? Just like that?"

He stops, his face a mask of indifference, but I see the irritation bubbling just under the surface. God help me, but I love making him lose his cool. Just a little. The guy doesn't flinch. He doesn't falter. He's too serious all the time. Too buttoned-up, and I don't like it.

For some reason, from the moment I saw him, I knew it was my job to loosen him up. I'd like it if I could make him a little more fun and happy, but I'm settling for that little vein in his temple to pulse and his body to grow so rife with tension that he gives me a verbal lashing.

I like what I like.

Don't judge me.

My blood races through my veins, full of excitement when he steps into me. His height matches my own, though I'd say I have about twenty pounds of solid muscle on him—but still, his stance is intimidating and sexy as all hell.

Yeah, I'm for sure in trouble here.

"Yes, Mr. Moore," he bites out, his voice clipped and stern. "Just like that. No. Absolutely not. I would never ask you to be a teacher's assistant for me. I have a week and a half left with you, and I'm counting down the days. After that, you're someone else's problem."

"I'd be an excellent TA. I'm top of the class without even having to try."

"And that's the problem, isn't it, Mr. Moore?" He glares at me. "You don't try. You don't take anything seriously enough to put any effort into anything. You take pride in absolutely nothing," he seethes, and my smirk falls, a frown taking it's spot. "So the answer is no. Have a good day."

He leaves me standing there in the hall, a cold feeling going through me from his words. But then, I take a deep breath and force my feet to keep walking.

He really doesn't like me. And that's fine. Totally fine.

I keep telling myself that all the way to my car that's in one of the lots near the building. Yes, I can easily walk to class, but I knew I'd feel like a drive after class and didn't want to go back to my place first.

And good thing too.

I'm wound tight, and I'm grateful I don't have any more classes today. But as I approach my brand-new, bright-blue Jeep Wrangler— thank you, Rhys and Blair—I stop short when I see Bree is here, leaning against the front.

I start walking again, picking up my pace as I approach her. "Bree? Are you okay? Is everyone okay?" I look around her frantically, panic setting in.

"Hey, everyone is fine," she says and places a hand on my shoulder to steady me. "Sorry. I didn't mean to scare you."

I try to brush that off but fail pretty quickly. Bree has no problem reading me, and after my little interaction with Professor Barlowe, I'm not in the mood to even try to keep up the charade. "So, everyone is okay?"

She nods at that and then gives me a really quick hug that I return before she releases me. "Yeah, everyone is fine."

"What brings you here then?" I ask lightly, not wanting her to think I don't want to see her. I always want to see Bree. Not only is she now my sister, she's been my best friend for over half my life.

"You're coming to my graduation, right?"

I lean against the front of my Jeep, sitting my ass right next to hers. "Of course I am. Wouldn't miss it." She nods slowly, but I know Bree— something is up. "What's wrong?" Is Blair driving you crazy with the planning?"

Bree grins, and I know that's exactly what's going on. "She means well."

I toss my head back and laugh about that. "She does."

"But oh my God, Fletch. She's invited so many people. I thought I made it clear to her I don't like people, but I guess not."

I laugh again because I can't help it. I think Bree might be even more antisocial than Rhett. "She knows. I swear. She's just wanting to make it perfect." I nudge Bree's small shoulder with my own. "I think this is probably hard for her. You're the last of the three leaving the nest."

Bree looks slightly guilty about that, and I feel like an asshole. That's not on her. And Blair is just as excited for Bree as she is sad that she's leaving. "I know it is. But she does have Max and Ian to dote all over now."

I grin. "She still trying to get them to wear matching outfits? Remember when she did that shit for our first family picture?"

Bree grins so big, I think it has to hurt her cheeks. "God, I love that woman."

"Me too," I say easily. "Guess a little out of control and way too many people in one place is worth having her in our lives."

"Oh, 100 percent," she laughs in agreement.

"So you drove an hour just to ask me that? There are these pretty cool things called phones. They send a message like magic. Don't even have to get in the car."

She shoves my shoulder. "Shut. Up. I'm actually meeting a friend in a few minutes and thought I'd stop by to see you first. Noticed your big ole blue gas sucker and decided to wait."

"You don't have friends."

She cackles at that. "Asshole." She shrugs. "Shana goes to school here too." I smile because Shana was the one friend besides Rhett and me she allowed around her in high school. And Shana was in Rhett's and my grade, so she graduated with us.

I eye her car, parked a few spots away from mine, and shake my head. Bree is very big on the environment. When I got the bigass Jeep, she asked for an electric car. "Admit it, you had to charge that little metal box you call a car, and that's really why you came to campus."

She flips me off and pushes off my bumper. "I'm glad you'll be at my party. You know she even invited Josh?" She pretends to gag, but I straight up tense at the name.

Josh was the closest thing Grayson had to a best friend in high school, and he totally made out with Bree at a party where they both had way too much to drink, and Bree accidentally drunkenly outed Grayson, right then and there.

But Josh was a lot cooler than we all thought and didn't miss a beat when he found out his friend was gay.

Of course, I kind of fucked up that summer and fooled around with him too. And Christmas break. Thankfully, it was not a love connection between Josh and Bree or I'd feel like a total asshole.

But the reason I'm tense is that Bree has no idea about any of it. No one does. Because once she knows about it, she'd be fine with it. Just like Blair. Probably totally inappropriate but fine. But when I open my mouth to tell her about it, I can't do it.

There's some sort of weird block there I hate. I internally curse myself, and Bree doesn't miss it. "You okay? You look pale."

I clear my throat and start to walk toward her car. She follows along. "I'm fine."

She unlocks her car and opens the door, climbing in. "Okay, well why don't you go get your big ass some food?"

I smile and nod. "Okay. I will. Be careful."

She waves to me. "See you at the party." She closes her door, and I wave before moving out of her way, so she can leave the lot.

As I walk back to my car, I'm surprised yet again as my favorite professor approaches the gray Lexus next to my Jeep. His hazel glare meets mine as I unlock my Jeep, loving that the beep sound is extra obnoxious.

"Nice car," I taunt him, opening my door.

"Thanks," he bites out, clearly not happy to see me. "My mommy and daddy didn't pay for it."

Prick.

He got me though. He gives me a cold smile before he climbs behind the wheel of his fancy ass car, starting it, then leaving the parking lot without another look in my direction.

Damn, I love seeing that little hint of fight he has in him.

Nothing hotter, in my opinion.

He thinks it pushes me away, but really, all it is, is a beacon to my fucked-up soul.

21

FLETCHER

The drive didn't really help. As much as I love messing with Professor Barlowe, I hate when he rattles me. And him dismissing me like he did today, for some reason, got to me.

But I nearly die of a heart attack when I unlock my apartment door and am instantly greeted by not my mom this time—no, this time it's Rhett doing the breaking and entering.

"Seriously?" I ask, tossing my keys on the table next to the door and trying to calm my racing pulse. "Do we need to establish some boundaries?" I ask as I make my way to the couch and sit next to him on the sofa, where he's made himself at home.

He gives a quick laugh. "Let's just call it payback. I believe you broke into my apartment a few times."

I grin because yes, yes I did. Our whole little makeshift family is totally free of boundaries.

"Where have you been?" he asks, and I sigh, tired from the day.

"Driving around."

"What's wrong?" He immediately becomes serious, and damn it, if there's anyone on this planet who knows me better than myself, it's Rhett. Blair, Rhys, and Bree know me well, but Rhett knows me the best.

"I have a professor who hates my guts."

Rhett is quiet for a moment. I know he doesn't miss when I go for a drive to nowhere, it's because I'm dealing with stuff. It's my little ritual. He sketches, but I drive with the music turned up loud on a path to nowhere. Just drive until I start to feel calm, or I give up and head home.

"And? That bothers you?" He sounds genuinely confused, and I laugh because yeah, people not liking me doesn't usually get to me. I couldn't give a flying fuck.

Usually.

I shrug. "He goes out of his way to remind me that he's better than me. That I'm just a kid he looks down on," I say, my voice thick with emotion I hate. "It's reminiscent of every motherfucker I ever met before Rhys and Blair."

He nods slowly because he gets it. We were told we weren't good enough for most of our lives. Passed around to different homes over and over again. "So he's a stuffy professor type. Fuck him."

I tense a little at that because yes, please.

I'd love to. And that's really damn confusing because he's not my type. I don't like rich, entitled people. I really don't. No matter how much I try to fit in with them, I want nothing to do with them.

I put on the show.

And no, Rhys and Blair don't count. Rhys was a foster kid, just like us. And Blair—well Blair is just cool as hell.

Rhett nudges my shoulder. "You know, if I didn't know any better, I'd say you have a crush."

I know he's trying to lighten the mood, and it works because I can't fight the grin that plays over my mouth. "And if I told you that I've been with a dude, would you still know better?"

Shit. That just came out. But I don't try to laugh it off or pull it back. I'm glad I said it.

I should have told him right away. "Are you fucking with me?" he asks carefully.

"So being with a guy is a joke?" I ask, keeping a totally straight face —and that shit is hard to do.

He sees right through it, though, and shoves my shoulder. "Quit being an asshole. You know it's not. So, you were with a guy?"

I nod, feeling pretty damn good to get it out. It shouldn't be a secret. I haven't held back in the past about hooking up with a chick, so I really shouldn't hold back now. "Just one."

"When?"

"Last summer. And over Christmas break."

Rhett seems to take in that information and then nods. "Okay. So you're . . ."

Ah, the label. Rhett took a long time to figure out his own. The poor guy struggled with it for a long time—even thought there was something wrong with him—until Grayson came along, breaking through those walls like an even more hyped-up version of the Kool Aid man and showing him he didn't need a label.

That there was nothing wrong with him and he was most certainly capable of love.

But we aren't the same. I'm not demisexual. I don't need a strong connection to feel sexual desire, and I'm pretty sure I'm as equally attracted to men as I am to women and have been for a while. "I think I'm bi."

He nods, not shocked at all. Not surprised. And he's not going to ask me a bunch of questions. Nope. Rhett just accepts it like I knew he would. "Cool."

"I think," I say because I've never said it out loud before.

He grasps the back of my neck with his hand, and I see the slight smile. "You like who you like when you like them. Nothing else matters."

I nod and smile too.

"Even if it's a prick professor, who's actually not nearly good enough for you and not the other way around."

I chuckle, and he releases me. "He's not so bad."

"Oh God, you have it bad, huh?" He laughs now, the tension leaving my body too.

"No. I just totally want to see him naked and find out what it's like to make him moan my name."

Rhett grimaces. "Too far. Way too far. You've been hanging out with Blair too much."

I laugh. "I even offered to be his TA."

"What?" Rhett sounds amused now.

"Yeah, but he told me *hell no*."

He studies me carefully for a moment, probably wondering what the hell is going on. I don't donate my time. I'm not like Rhett. He loves to volunteer. I've been to the city mission where he volunteers a few times with him before, but it's not a big thing for me.

I tutor for cash. I never sign up for extra work though. But I was dead serious about being a TA for him. I don't even know how the process works or if it's a paid or credit position. I just loved the idea of *assisting* the grumpy bastard.

"So why are you here?" I ask, pulling out my phone to order something for dinner.

"Eh, Grayson had an evening class, and I knew Bree was coming up here. Thought I might come hang out."

"You worried about Bree?" I ask, amused because she can take care of herself, but that doesn't mean we aren't protective of her.

"She took it hard when we left last year."

I stiffen at that. "Hard how?"

He shrugs. "I don't know. I think she felt like we were abandoning her. And I've tried to be more present since, you know? But she's got something going on."

"You think Shana and she are . . . ?"

He shakes his head. "Nah. I don't think she likes her that way, but something seems off."

Maybe I need to do better at checking in too. I always thought of Bree as untouchable, nothing ever scared her. She was braver than Rhett and me combined, but if Rhett thinks something is off, it probably is.

"Should we call her and guilt her into coming over here?"

Rhett holds up his phone. "Already sent a text about a fucked-up-adopted-siblings get-together."

I laugh at that, and when Bree shows up a couple of hours later to eat pizza and watch trash horror movies that are edited for television with us, everything feels right with the world.

It's always been that way with these two.

RONAN

"You did not agree to that." I stare at Annie, trying like crazy not to lose my shit. There's no way she would do this.

"Look, I'm sorry, but I did." She at least has the decency to look guilty after admitting she took Fletcher Moore on as a TA for next semester. Fletcher. Moore. The bane of my existence.

"What the hell were you thinking?"

"I wasn't," she says quickly. "He looked at me with those big blue eyes of his and pouted at me. Before I knew it, I was saying yes." I hardly believe she didn't think about it very seriously though. I know Annie. She thinks about everything, but I don't understand how she could have said yes.

"He's very convincing," Nathan butts in.

I don't normally get angry with my two best friends, but right now, I'm completely furious with Annie. "How could you agree to that? And do not tell me you have a crush on the eternal child," I growl. The thought makes me sick to my stomach. She's smarter than this.

She rolls her eyes at me and waves me off. "Pretty sure my wife would have something to say about that."

I bite my tongue and don't throw out there the very *real* controversy going around campus with a married professor because I know, without a doubt, Annie is 100 percent committed to her marriage. "Well . . ."

"Well nothing. Yes, I'm an out and proud bisexual, and he's very pretty to look at. No, I don't do anything based on looks alone, and he's a damn fetus. And I'm happily married. I would never do anything to fuck that up. While he's stupid hot—"

"He's not." I feel the need to argue.

She doesn't miss a beat. "He is, but I'm not attracted to him in the slightest. He's pretty to look at, but that's not what I meant when I said he flashed those big eyes and pout and it worked. There's something deeper inside Fletcher."

"There's not," I argue again. "Nothing at all. He played you, like he plays everyone. He doesn't need to be a damn TA." I cannot believe she fell for his charm, that anyone would fall for his charm. It's beyond ridiculous to me.

"I think he does," Annie says, putting her foot down hard. "I know you think he's a spoiled brat—" she starts, and again I rudely interrupt her.

"He is. Those ridiculous tank tops he wears? They're like a hundred dollars. For a scrap of material."

"Okay, grandpa," she says and pats my shoulder. I huff, and she goes on, "He seemed to really want this. And he's smart. I'd be an idiot to pass up an excellent assistant like him. And besides, he seems to need a challenge." She takes a bite of the salad she's been picking at while we're at lunch at our favorite café near campus. I was enjoying the damn lunch, too, until she dropped this bomb on me. "And a challenge I will give him."

I have no doubt she will, but I can't believe she told Fletcher yes. I don't imagine he hears *no* all that often. "Really? In *sociology*?"

She frowns at me. "Dick."

I grin at that, but I'm still angry. Well, not really angry. She can do whatever she wants, but I'm not happy he's going to be her TA. That it's very likely I'll see him in her office—which is right next to mine. And I'll see him on campus because the sociology building is right next to the economics building. It's a small damn campus. "Good luck next semester then. Nothing is going to get done."

"Do you want to talk about why you hate this kid so damn much?" Annie asks, and Nathan rests his chin on his hand, propped up on the table, waiting for my answer.

"I don't hate him."

"You do," they both say, and I bristle.

"I don't," I say quickly. "I just . . ."

"You had to work hard for every single thing, and he has it easy. Or appears to," Annie supplies.

I roll my eyes but hate that she's nailed it. "Can you blame me?" I've watched spoiled kids like him my whole life. Taking everything for granted. Lazing around while I was working my ass off just to survive.

She shrugs and takes another bite of her salad. "Yes. I can because you're a smart man, Ronan. You can't let this get to you. He's a good kid who wants to help. There's nothing wrong with that, and he's smart as hell."

"Just because he reads for fun," I grumble.

She tosses a crouton at me from across the table, and I open my mouth just in time to catch it and chew. She laughs and rolls her eyes at me. "Very nice." I shrug and swallow before she goes on, "I like the kid. I think you should give him a chance. There's more to him than what we see in class."

"There really isn't," I say again, being totally petulant, but damn it, she can't be right about this. "He was finally going to be out of my hair. One week left, and then it's just a final."

She doesn't look sympathetic in the slightest. "And he still is. He's no longer your student. Not your assistant either. Not your problem, Ronan."

"But he'll be around."

"You sound like a child," she shoots back at me, and I hate how disappointed she looks at me right now. I know I'm being ridiculous. I know that, but I can't help it.

There's something about Fletcher that makes me want him as far away from me as possible.

As soon as possible.

And thanks to my dear friend, Annie, that won't be so soon now.

FLETCHER

Bree is a high-school graduate. I can't believe it. I mean, she's smart as hell, but still, there was a time when I didn't think any of us would get here. I'm in college. Rhett is a tattoo artist after graduating from high school, and now Bree is a high-school graduate and going to college.

That is, if she'd make up her mind about where she's going. She's been awfully dodgy about the question for a while now but especially today. And believe me, a lot of people asked her that very question today.

She always makes some excuse and just walks off. I asked Blair about it, who said she hasn't officially enrolled anywhere yet. I can tell Blair is getting twitchy about it and can't blame her.

But the party guests are long gone tonight, and when I sneak down into the kitchen to grab something to eat, I'm surprised to see Bree walking in through the kitchen door. Well, more like stumbling through the door.

"Shit," she curses when she trips but catches herself before actually falling.

"Bree?"

"Holy fuck," she gasps and places a hand over her heart. "What are you doing down here in the middle of the night?"

I size her up—she's wearing the same thing she had on at the party —t-shirt and tattered jeans with her favorite tennis shoes—but her long hair is a little tousled and even in the low light of the kitchen nightlight above the stove, I can see she's wasted. "I was hungry. Now you."

She waves me off and closes the door before walking further into the kitchen and closer to me. "I was celebrating." I can smell the alcohol on her breath but don't call her on it. It's not like I didn't party a little, here and there, in high school.

"You okay, Bree?" I ask her instead because I know she's not. I can feel it. Rhett was definitely right. Something is up.

"I'm fine. I'm going to bed."

She starts to walk past me, but I gently reach for her wrist. "Bree, talk to me," I plead with her, using my eyes.

She doesn't really fall for it like most people do, but she sighs heavily and drops her shoulders, pulling her wrist from my grip. "I'm fine, Fletcher."

"Are you?" Rhett's deep voice causes us both to turn around at the same time, seeing him standing there in his tank top and shorts, his hair all messed up from sleep—or his boyfriend, Grayson. Don't really want to think about that.

"Oh my God," Bree exclaims, but she keeps her voice to a harsh whisper. "No. I don't need the big-brother routine from you two. I'm fine."

"I mean, we are your brothers. And we are older," Rhett says as he walks further into the kitchen and stands next to me. We stand shoulder to shoulder, our arms crossed, as we face Bree. "And it's not an act or routine, Bree. We care about you."

She waves him off, and it hurts. My heart actually pangs when she waves that off. "We do," I say firmly.

She pulls in a deep breath and lets it out in a rush. "I know you both care about me, but you have your own lives. I'm fine. I don't need you guys to take care of me. I never did."

That stings too. "I thought we always took care of each other," I say, hating that I'm letting this get to me. I want to make a joke. Brush it off. But I can't. These two have seen me at my worst. They know about most of the things I've been through.

She looks slightly guilty at that, her eyes going from mine to Rhett's and then back to me. "I got into New York."

Rhett and I stare at each other for a moment before I look back at Bree. "Bree! That's fantastic news. Why the hell are you so salty?"

I go to hug her, truly happy for her, but she holds her hands up to stop me. I don't know what her problem is. Bree wants to go into interior design. She loves it. You wouldn't think so, but she does, and she has a real eye for it. And she's had her eye on this prestigious college in New York for years. "I can't go."

"What?" My jaw drops as I lower my hands, giving up on hugging her.

Rhett takes a step forward. "What do you mean you can't go? This is your dream, Bree."

"It is." She seems to sober up a little bit and goes over to the sink, grabbing a cup and filling it with water. She takes a big swig as Rhett and I turn to look at her head-on. Waiting for her reply. She places the cup back down on the counter and leans against it, her eyes full of sadness. "But I can't leave them. After all they did for us, I can't just pick up and leave. Go to New York."

She shakes her head as if that idea is insane. I know she's talking about Blair and Rhys, but I don't understand why she feels that way. "Blair and Rhys are going to be thrilled. They want the best for you."

"You know they do, Bree," Rhett adds.

"They do, but I can't leave them like you two shitheads did." Bree hits back, and my eyebrows jump up to my hairline.

"I didn't leave them." I point at Rhett. "And he still lives in the same damn town as them. We're growing up, Bree. It happens."

She scoffs at that and then points at Rhett. "He left Rhys." Her voice has no venom in it, it's more sad. But I wince anyway because I know that was hard for Rhett to decide to work for someone else at their tattoo shop instead of at Rhys's already established, very successful one. But Rhett needed to make his own way.

"Don't do that," I say firmly.

Rhett puts his hand on my shoulder and shakes his head at me. "I did what I needed to do. It hurt like hell, and I felt like I was letting him down. But you know what? Rhys wasn't mad or upset with me. He was proud that I was doing this on my own. And he'll be happy for you too, Bree. They don't want you to put your life on hold for them."

"I'm sorry I said that, Rhett." And I can tell she means it. "We just . . ." She lifts her eyes, and I see the profound conflict in them. "They rescued us. Isn't it a slap in the face to go across the country?"

"No. It absolutely is not." All three of us startle this time at the sound of Blair's voice, and when I look toward the edge of the kitchen, I see she's not alone. Rhys is firmly by her side.

Bree walks back over to where Rhett and I are standing, moving between us as she faces our parents. "Oh, you are in so much trouble," I taunt, and she elbows me in the side.

"Shut up."

I can't help laughing, but stop when Blair and Rhys approach, Blair stepping closer than Rhys and grasping Bree's cheeks in her hands. "Bree, you got in, and you didn't tell us?"

"I wasn't going to go," Bree says, her voice strained with tight emotion. "I don't want to leave you all."

My heart breaks, thinking about her going that far away, but I know this is important to her. Which makes it important to all of us.

"You won't be leaving us," Blair says with that confident smile. "I know how to book a flight, and if you think I won't be stalking your life just as much as I stalk these two,"—she gestures toward Rhett and me, and we both smile before she continues, her eyes on Bree— "you're crazy, kiddo."

Bree sniffs, and Rhys walks up next to Blair, placing his hand on her shoulder. "We love you, Bree. If you want to go—and we all know you do—you should. We aren't going anywhere. We'll be here when you're ready to come back." He gives a half smile, which is massive for Rhys. "If you come back."

Blair nods easily. "Or I'll just have to pack up the whole family and move us all up there."

"Oh, God," I groan. "Bree you better come back someday because I'm not moving to New York."

She smiles brightly at me then, and I laugh because we all know if that's what we must do, we'll do it.

Blair hugs Bree close to her. "I love all of you, but you're totally insane if you think you're getting away from me."

Bree sniffs and lets Blair hold her. "I'm sorry I didn't tell you. I knew you'd make me go."

Blair pulls back enough to look Bree in the eyes. "Do you want to go?"

Bree bites her bottom lip for a moment, taking a brief pause before she nods her head slowly. "It's my dream."

Blair kisses her on the forehead and smiles as she does it. "Then it's our dream too. We're gonna make it happen." She hugs Bree again, and then we all wind up in a weird sort of group hug. With the non-touchers—Rhys and Rhett—awkwardly on the outside, it works for us.

Afterward, Rhys makes grilled cheese for all of us, and Blair makes hot chocolate before we sit around the kitchen table, talking about everything under the sun.

We keep it down, so we don't wake Grayson, Max, and Ian, but still, it's a damn good time.

Reminiscent of the many times we did this over the years. And there really were many. Anytime anyone couldn't sleep, we'd wind up right here. Talking everything out.

I have no idea how the hell I got so damn lucky, but regardless of what anyone thinks, I'll never take this for granted.

RONAN

It's finally summer. Don't get me wrong, I love my job, but there's something about summer in a college town. There are still enough people to keep the town running, but it's much, much less.

And while I still teach a couple of classes in the summer, I have a little bit more free time. So today, I decided to meet Annie for coffee at one of my favorite shops near campus. She's in a hurry this morning, so we only have a little time to chat while we wait for our orders. Thanks to most of the students going back home for the summer, there's hardly any wait. Still, it's always good to catch up with her, especially since it's been over a week since finals, and I haven't seen Nathan or her much.

But I quickly realize I was just too damn happy this morning as a familiar figure saunters inside the small coffee shop. His hair looks like he just rolled out of bed—but somehow is still neat and looks clean and fresh. He's wearing one of those tank tops that cost far too much and clings way too close to his chiseled body. It's already warm this morning, so I suppose he's appropriately dressed.

"Well, good morning, Professor Briggs." He smiles big at Annie before turning his blue gaze on me. "*Professor* Barlowe."

See, why does he have to emphasize *professor* only when he's talking to me? Always trying to rile me up.

Annie just laughs at his antics. "Good morning, Fletcher. How's the summer going?"

I hate that she's engaging him. That they have a whole rapport because they already set up his TA gig, and when the fall semester starts, he'll be working with her. "It's going pretty well. Just lounging around."

I roll my eyes, and Annie nudges me. "Well, I'm sorry, but I have to get going." She holds up both her hands, full with two coffees and a bag of muffins. "Don't want to keep the wife waiting."

"No time to chitchat today?" I tease, and she just winks at me.

"Hell no. Wifey gets hangry." She waves to me and then to Fletcher. "I'll see you around, Fletcher. Give 'em hell."

I frown, and Fletcher only grins widely, giving her a wave. "Will do."

She leaves, and I start toward the door far away from Fletcher. "Aw, come on, Professor. No time to chitchat? It's summer, and I'm pretty sure you don't have a wife." His eyes go to my left hand. "At least, you don't wear a ring."

"I'm not married." *Damn it. Why did I need to say that?* I don't owe him any personal details. "And I was just here to meet my friend. We . . ."—I motion between our bodies—"are not friends."

"We could be."

"No. We can't." I start to move past him again, but his big body blocks my exit. "Have a good day, Mr. Moore," I try to dismiss him.

No such luck. "Would it really kill you to have a cup of coffee with me?" The way he says it doesn't sound innocent at all, and the way he's looking at me tells me he doesn't mean for it to.

"Yes. I think it might. You're not great for my blood pressure."

He throws his head back and laughs at that. It's a genuine, real laugh. A light melody my ears don't seem to hate as much as I'd like them to. *Damn ears.* I mean, this kid drives me crazy. His laugh should too. But it's a truly beautiful sound. And when his eyes meet mine, the laughter still dancing in them, I'm tempted to agree, but then something shifts.

It happens so fast, I nearly miss what he's reacting to.

But I vaguely recognize the sound of a small child throwing a tantrum, along with the rough, almost condescending voice of a parent, either at their wits end or who just never had it under control in the first place—I can't speculate which.

But it doesn't seem to matter to Fletcher either way. As the parent shouts at the child and makes the kid cry more, Fletcher has gone nearly catatonic.

His big body is frozen, except for rapid breaths racking his form, and his eyes are a desert of emotion. "Fletcher," I say firmly, but he doesn't see me.

It's like he doesn't see anyone.

What the hell is going on?

The child and the parent head out of the coffee shop. The child has stopped crying and may have gotten their way because it seems awfully content as the frazzled parent follows behind. But Fletcher hasn't moved.

"Fletcher," I try again, but he's just stuck.

Damn it. I move closer to him, my coffee in one hand but using the other hand to cup his cheek gently.

"Fletcher," I breathe out, suddenly terrified for him. I don't like it, but I really don't have time to worry about that. "Fletcher, look at me." My thumb grazes gently under his eye.

Finally, he slowly comes back, his eyes meeting mine, but he's still in a daze when he opens his mouth to speak. "You're touching me."

"What?" I breathe out as I stare into his startling blue eyes and barely register his words.

I see a hint of playfulness come back to his eyes, and a small smile forms on his full lips. "You're touching me."

It finally clicks, and I quickly drop my hand away from his face. "Oh shit. Sorry."

I'm flustered, which I really, really hate, but it doesn't bother Fletcher. No, he seems to be right back to himself now, his grin growing wide. "Didn't say I didn't like it." His tone is light and playful, and he actually winks at me, all that mischief flooding right back. "I just said you were touching me."

I huff and take a step back from him. "What was that all about?" I ask, my eyes searching his as I wait for his answer.

An answer I know isn't coming as soon as I see the way his smile has transformed. It's not playful. He's not flirting. No. He's putting on a show. He's got a big fake, plastic smile on his all too handsome face. "Nothing."

I need to just go. This man is beyond infuriating, and I don't have the time or patience for him. "Fletcher . . ." I start, needing the answer and not knowing why. "What happened? You were frozen."

"I'm fine," he says, that enraging smile firmly on his face.

"You can tell me," I say and mentally kick myself. That is so not the way to get him out of my life and mind. By letting him know I'm here for him. That he can talk to me.

I don't want to see more in him. I want him to be this rich, spoiled brat who doesn't have a care in the world. But that look on his face. The way he couldn't seem to move. He looked so damn lost in that moment.

How many times did I look that way over the years?

"It was nothing. Don't worry, Professor . . ." He leans into me just so slightly, his eyes boring into mine. "I'm just a simple rich boy. It doesn't go deeper than that."

I glare at him, wanting that to be true. "Yeah well, things aren't always what they seem."

He smirks at that, his eyes flashing with something I can't quite pin down, and he shrugs his large shoulders. "You have me all figured out, Professor. Don't worry." He looks up toward the coffee counter and then back at me. "Sorry, I actually don't feel like chatting today. Or coffee. I think I'll just head out."

Before I can argue with him or ask him again about what happened, he ducks out of the coffee shop and starts jogging down the street, like it was his plan all along. But my mind is stuck on that haunted look on his face.

What the hell was that all about?

FLETCHER

Yeah, that did not go as planned. Not even close. Jesus fuck, what the hell was that? Why does the universe seem to hate me?

I swear, when I saw my favorite professor through the window of the coffee shop as I was jogging by, I was thanking that universe. But now, as I'm running out of the shop, I realize it was just a cruel trick.

I'm embarrassed and unstable as I run back to my apartment, but instead of going inside, I climb in my Jeep and behind the wheel. I turn up the music and head for the highway, trying to clear out my head.

I don't want to think about what happened. I hate that he witnessed it. It was a kid throwing a tantrum and a parent getting angry. It happens every single day. I'm sure that kid was just fine.

But I can't seem to make my mind believe that, and my heart is racing as I drive, turning the music up a little louder. My phone beeps with a notification, and I glance at it to see it's a text from Bree.

She's in town.

I take a deep breath and turn off the highway, going toward one of my favorite spots. When I reach the lake, I park my Jeep, grab my phone, and hop out, finding a large rock to sit on as I look out at the water.

I text Bree and ask her to meet me here. She's been here a couple of times with me. It's a spot I found my first week of college when the jumble of so many *normal* kids in one place was too damn much for my brain.

I wound up on a drive after my first class where I found this place, and when Bree visited me a few weekends later, I brought her out here to show her. She shows up about an hour later, just her, even though I'm sure she's in town to stay with Shana. She must have sensed I didn't want to be around anyone else.

She joins me on the same rock I'm sitting on, leaning her head on my shoulder. "What's wrong, Fletch?"

I shrug, lifting her head a little bit as I move the shoulder she's resting on. "I just needed to go for a drive."

"Right," she says, not believing that for a second. "What happened?" I like that she doesn't waste any time. She gets to the point and doesn't put up with my bullshit. She's one of the few who won't.

I look out at the beautiful water, hoping it will calm me. Maybe I should have chosen the library instead. The drive didn't help, and the water doesn't seem to either this time. "I was totally fine, Bree." I shake my head sadly. "I was flirting with this hot professor who hates me—"

"Okay, we're for sure coming back to that part later," she interrupts with a laugh.

I smile, figuring she wouldn't let that part go, but my mood is still darkened by what happened. "I heard this kid throwing a fit. You know, totally normal tantrum to get what they wanted."

I feel her nod against my shoulder as she listens.

"But then the dad yelled at the kid. His deep voice—he sounded so damn angry. So mad." I feel her stiffen, but she doesn't say anything. "I just froze. Completely. My heart was racing, and it was like I couldn't breathe. It was just a dad angry at his kid for throwing a fit in public, but I . . ."

My heart rate starts to speed up again, and I curse myself for not being able to control it.

"Fletch . . ." she says as she pulls back from my shoulder, and I turn to look at her as she turns her body to face me. I can feel her concern.

"Don't. I'm fine." I try to quickly shut her down.

But Bree doesn't back down from anything. "Are you?" she asks so simply, but there's nothing simple about her question.

"Bree . . ." I groan, but again, she doesn't budge.

She's brave. Always has been. Lifting her chin and looking me right in the eyes. "We all had trauma. We were all in horrible places, off and on, but . . ." Her chin wobbles slightly, and her voice cracks. "I know no one ever actually put their hands on me."

"Bree . . ." I plead, my eyes closing because I don't want to talk about this. I never want to talk about this.

"But I still hear it. I can still feel like what it was like before," she whispers.

I open my eyes and let out a deep breath, noticing that her eyes are watery as she stares at me. I know she does. I know we all do. Our lives have been so damn good since we went to live with Rhys and Blair. So damn . . . effortless.

That sometimes we can fool ourselves into forgetting what it was like before we met them. Of being bounced around from home to home. When some really weren't that bad, but they still weren't a real home for us. When some were godawful.

And no, thankfully, as far as I know with Bree, no one touched her. Or Rhett. I wasn't so lucky. The last foster home I was in was a goddamn nightmare. It was what really forced Rhys and Blair into taking Rhett and me on.

I'll never forget them showing up in their fancy car in the crappiest neighborhood. I was just sitting on the porch with a black eye, hating life. Wanting to run away. My foster father still screaming at me as he walked around inside, tossing shit on a drunken rampage.

I was his favorite punching bag, but I told myself it wasn't so bad. That his house was pretty close to where Rhett was staying. That Bree was happy and settled with Rhys and Blair already. That I didn't want to shake everything up.

But then there they were. They pulled up and scooped me out of hell.

"I'm okay, Bree."

She reaches up and cups my cheek, similar to the way Professor Barlowe did only hours ago. This touch is different though. It's comforting, but even through the haze of my panic attack when Barlowe touched me, I could feel the heat. The spark of his firm yet gentle, commanding touch.

I lean into Bree for a moment and then take her hand in mine. "I really am okay. I hate when this happens, I do. It's fucking embarrassing."

She shakes her head. "There's nothing to be embarrassed about."

I wave that off because yeah, I'm embarrassed as hell. "I'm okay. I just needed to . . ." To what? Push it all away, I guess. Take some time with it? I don't really know.

She squeezes my hand and then lays her head back on my shoulder. "If you need anything . . . if you need to talk to someone . . ."

"I'm talking to someone right now," I say with a smile.

I can feel her shaking her head. "You know what I mean."

I do. Blair had us all going to therapy for a while. She wanted to make sure we were okay, and I understood that, though, it didn't do much for me. Bree still goes though, and I'm happy as hell that it seems to work for her. "I do, and I really don't need therapy or pills. I have it under control."

"We all deal with it in our own way," she says, and I hear no judgment in her tone. None whatsoever because she knows.

"If I ever feel like I don't have it under control, I'll get help. I promise."

She nods again. "I know you will."

We're quiet for a while, just staring out at the lake with her lying her head on my shoulder and my arm around her. Some people may question whether the love between us ever crossed a line, since we aren't blood-related, and while Bree is gorgeous, it's never been like that between us.

Not ever. She's always been my little sister from the day we met.

And there was a time when she was in love with Rhett. Like actual love. But he didn't feel the same about her. I know that hurt her, but I think she realized it never would have worked between them.

That Rhett was meant for Grayson. And she seems content these days—especially since she finally told us about going to New York. "Blair driving you crazy with planning?"

She laughs. "Not really. She's so damn excited, Fletch."

I grin. "She loves you."

"She loves us all," she says simply, and yeah, she really does. There's no denying that.

I think that's another way I chase away the bad memories. She's placed so many good ones over the bad.

"So, this hot professor?" Bree prompts, and I bark out a quick laugh because, oh yeah, I kind of let that slip, and of course she isn't going to let that go.

"He hates me, Bree."

"He?" she asks, but there really isn't any surprise there. Or any judgment. Not that I would expect there to be from her.

"Yes, _he_," I state firmly, happy to finally be talking about this with her too.

"Huh," she says and then leans up to look at my face. "So I don't want to assume because I'm not an asshole, but since I've seen your tongue shoved down more women's throats than I'd like . . ." She shudders, and I roll my eyes and laugh.

"I'm into both," I answer the question she never really got to. "I'm bisexual."

"Cool," she says effortlessly and lays her head back down on my shoulder.

"Yeah, I mean, I think I'm into both genders equally. I haven't really figured out my exact Kinsey Scale score, but I think I'm pretty firmly in the middle."

She laughs and shakes her head at me. "I'm not at all surprised that you've overanalyzed the hell out of your sexuality."

I chuckle, but yeah, I like research. When I first realized I had an attraction to a guy at school, I went right on the internet and read.

And read some more. Not because I thought it was wrong, but I guess because it made it seem even more normal to know that hell, there's even an actual scale out there for sexuality.

Pretty damn cool, if you ask me.

"Speaking of that scale . . ." I start, and she looks at me, raising an eyebrow as she waits for the question. "You and Shana?"

She grins at that but doesn't seem surprised. "Nope. We're just friends, for real. I think I may be the only mostly straight one out of the bunch. But if I fall for a girl, I won't fight it, that's for damn sure."

I grin. "Mostly?"

She shrugs. "Like I said, I won't fight it. If my soulmate happens to be a woman, then that's how it's supposed to be."

"You're pretty fucking cool, Bree."

She laughs. "So are you. Please remember that."

I nod slowly, knowing what she's trying to tell me.

That no matter what I went through before, I'm really okay now.

And I'm trying everything I can to make sure I believe that.

RONAN

It's been a week since Fletcher ran out of the coffee shop, and I can't stop thinking about him. It's driving me insane.

I don't understand what the hell happened, and I'm an overthinker. That's all. I just like to know the answer to a question, and he didn't answer it for me. That's why I can't stop thinking about it.

That's the lie I continue to tell myself as I walk into the campus library. It's a nice evening, and I was out for a walk, drawn to the beautiful stone building. I figured why not go in and check things out.

And I see Fletcher right away.

It's almost empty in here, and he's massive, so of course it's not hard to spot him. But how the hell is he here? Tonight, of all nights, when I decide to walk in here. It makes no sense, and my legs take me straight to him.

Angry for absolutely no reason, I stop only a foot away from where he's reading quietly in a chair by the window. "Professor."

"No," I say instantly. "Don't call me that."

He quirks one brow at me, clearly amused, and damn it, that annoys me too. "What should I call you?"

Damn him. He's having way too much fun with this, and he's back to being the annoying ass who used to come into my class, all late and unbothered. "Just . . ." I'm flustered. Goddammit, I'm flustered. I hate that. "What are you doing here?"

He looks around the practically deserted room and then lifts the book he's reading up. It looks like a biography of some sort maybe. Definitely not a textbook. "Reading," he supplies the obvious answer.

"No." I say again, and that word just seems to be stuck in my head. "You don't just come to the library during the summer to read. No."

He stands up slowly, creeping into my space, but I don't back up. I don't relent, even though I know I should. "Libraries are my favorite place."

"Bullshit," I whisper-hiss.

Instead of being amused, he looks slightly irritated now. That's new. "Are you saying I'm lying? What the hell would I get out of lying?"

I scoff loudly at that and fold my arms over my chest, hating how agitated I feel. "Are you kidding? How about to rile me up? Which seems to be your number-one goal in life." I say far too loudly, and I finally realize just how close we're standing and drop my arms to my sides, taking one step back. "You know what? Nope. I'm not doing this. It doesn't matter."

I notice him visibly flinch at that, but I can't dwell on it.

"Have a good night, Mr. Moore." I turn and rush out of the library, hating that whole scene. What if anyone saw that? What would they think? Me practically yelling at a student in the library for reading.

I really need to get a grip. I get all the way to the edge of the parking lot and notice he's caught up to me. "What's your deal with me? Why the hell do you hate me so much?"

His large body is in front of mine, and it appears as if no one else is on campus. It's dark out, but several streetlights illuminate the space. And I can see he looks upset. Really upset.

"I don't hate you," I say because of course I don't. I don't know him well enough to hate him. That's ridiculous. "Laziness and entitlement bug the shit out of me. They're my two biggest pet peeves," I continue, and I notice his smile is completely gone now, replaced by a dark glare.

"I'm not lazy," he says firmly, his body moving closer to mine, pushing me back a little so I have to step backward off the curb and into the actual parking lot. I don't stumble though. "I may be spoiled, but I'm not lazy."

I study him carefully, trying to examine his expression in the low lighting. He seems deadly serious, and I wonder why the lazy part bugs him so much but not the spoiled part. "You act like you don't have a care in the world. You don't seem to study or care about school. You saunter in with the biggest air of arrogance I've ever seen. You don't seem to have any goals other than to drive me insane."

"Fuck. You," he says, crowding into my space and making me take another step back. My ass hits the car behind me, which I quickly realize is his blue Jeep.

I'm surprised by the venom in his words, his eyes shooting daggers at me. "Careful, Mr. Moore, it seems that smile you work so hard to put on your face every day is slipping."

"Tell me what your problem is with me." I can feel his body heat. He's standing close, and I don't push him away like I should.

"I already told you," I bite out, and he winces—it's slight, but I see it.

"I'm not lazy," he says again, with a broken tone in his voice I don't like as much as I want to. I should want to break him. That way he'll leave me alone. *Right?*

"Who the hell are you?" I ask angrily. "You make no sense whatsoever."

And he doesn't. He's an enigma, if I've ever seen one.

"Why do you care?" he asks me, his eyes boring into my own, his big body nearly pressed up against mine. I should shove him back. Tell him to keep his damn distance. Anyone could see us and question just what the hell is going on, but I don't make a move to push him away.

"Because you saunter into my classroom with expensive clothes and so much damn *I don't give a fuck* attitude, it makes me want to scream. Your arrogance is unmatched." He looks like he's about to argue, but I don't give him the time. "But then you freak the hell out when you see a child getting reprimanded, and you read in libraries for fun. You make no sense. So I ask, who the hell are you?" My chest puffs in and out with fury.

"I'm no one!" he yells, surprising me. I'm not used to seeing Fletcher shaken. "You cracked it wide-open. I was born a no one. My own parents didn't want me. Just tossed me away and hoped for the best." I stand there, shocked stupid as Fletcher goes on, "Or I think so. I actually have no idea because I spent the next decade in foster care before the woman who I wish I was born to came and rescued me from hell." My knees nearly buckle, and I feel dizzy as I listen to the words coming from him. "And yeah, I let her spoil me. I wanted it. I liked it. I never had that before, and Blair was the best damn thing that ever happened to me. But my past is always there, haunting me." He steps even closer to me, the fake smile and fuckboy attitude long gone, his jaw gritted, and anger flaring in his eyes. "And there will always be people like you reminding me that I'm no one."

I shake my head in disbelief. "You were in foster care?" I barely manage, my throat dry and my mind foggy.

"Yeah, I was." He stands so close to me, I can feel his breath on my face. He leans in even closer, his lips near my ear. "I like libraries because they were the only safe place for me as a kid. When it all got to be too damn much, I could go to the library, crack open a book, and forget the rest of the world."

He starts to pull back after that, but I mess up and grasp his forearm with my hand. His eyes lock on mine, and I can't seem to form any words. Fletcher was in foster care, and from the sounds of it, I don't think it was good at all.

Only safe space.

I don't think. I can't seem to, but the only thing I want in this moment is to comfort him. To shield him from the pain I have no doubt is front and center after talking about his past.

I tug him into me and before I know it, my lips are slamming against his. He grunts in surprise, but it only lasts a second because before I know what's happening, we're in a duel for dominance. His mouth attacks mine, and his tongue is tangling with my own. It's a fierce kiss, more intense than I've ever experienced, and it sets my entire being on fire.

He doesn't pull out of my hold. But his free hand moves to my hair, tugging at the strands, tilting my head back as he continues to plunder my mouth. My lips are swollen and sore but blissfully so as we kiss. My hand moves from his forearm, up his bare bicep, and I revel in the tight muscles.

I need to stop. I know this. Somewhere in the back of my mind, it registers that we're on campus right now. But I can't seem to remove my lips from his long enough to do that. We're fused together, his hard body against mine as his fingers grip my hair and tug ever so slightly, just this side of pain.

I love every second of it.

But all too soon, he's the one who's pulling back. Not too far though. His forehead rests against mine as we pant desperately. "Come with me."

My first reaction is yes. I want that so damn bad.

But then, reality comes crashing back. We're on campus. Anyone could see us like this. His hand is still in my hair, mine on his upper arm. Our bodies pressed together.

"Fletcher . . ." I try to keep my voice even and firm but not cruel. He may drive me insane, but I'm starting to realize maybe I had him semi-wrong. He's not just a spoiled rich kid. Or at least he wasn't born that way. "I could lose my job."

"No," he says just as firmly, his forehead still resting against mine as he shakes his head. "I'm not a student. It's summer. Just come with me."

"You *are* a student," I argue weakly. Every part of me wants to go with him, and I don't even know where he wants to go.

"I'm not enrolled in any classes at the moment."

He makes it sound so easy. So damn simple. "Fletcher . . ." I say, still off-kilter after that life-altering kiss that can never happen again.

I'm a professor. He's a student. It really is that black and white. He drops his hand from my hair and then lifts his head to look into my eyes, and I see the stubbornness in them. Stubbornness I thought was arrogance, but maybe now, I see it differently.

Just from one simple admission. Because it's not simple at all.

Fletcher was in foster care. His parents abandoned him at a young age, and if anyone knows what that's like, it's me.

It's anything but simple.

"I'm not your student. I'm never taking Econ again, if I can help it. No offense Professor, but that shit is boring as fuck."

Damn it. A quick burst of laughter leaves my lips, and I shake my head. "Where? I ask.

"Just a drive."

My tongue darts out, licking over my sore, now-dry lips, and I swear I can still taste him there. I notice his eyes tracking the movement, but he doesn't make another move to kiss me.

"Okay."

His eyes light up, and I hate and love that at the same time. Who knew I'd delight in making this man happy? Certainly not me.

He doesn't gloat though. He just unlocks his Jeep, and we both climb inside before he takes off on our drive.

It's just a drive.

This is totally okay.

Totally. Fine.

FLETCHER

He kissed me. We kissed.

Did that really happen? I'd think it was a really hot dream if it weren't for the fact that the man is sitting next to me in my Jeep right now. He's not looking at me or saying anything, and that's okay with me.

I just turn up the radio and head for my spot. Why? I have no idea.

I can't believe I told him about my past as a foster kid, and I'm not really sure why I did, except I couldn't take him calling me lazy. How many times did my worthless, cruel foster parents shout at me, calling me lazy? How many nights did I stay up afraid and alone, making me so damn tired the next day, I could barely move? Only to be shouted at and called names.

I couldn't handle it from him.

I just couldn't. It was like I needed him to know.

And the way he reacted? It was with total shock. He had no idea. And I guess that makes sense. I work really hard so no one sees. I put up a great facade as the arrogant spoiled kid without a care in the world. I'm happy for people to see me that way. I want them to. Anything but knowing the truth.

But not him. I couldn't take him looking at me like that any longer.

We make it to my spot, and I don't waste any time, turning off the Jeep and climbing out, hoping he'll follow me. Thankfully, he does. And when I sit down on my rock, he takes a seat next to me.

"You were in foster care?" His deep voice is a quiet rumble at my side.

I nod, but it's dark out, and I know he can't see my face. For that, I'm grateful. I don't want him to see the way it still haunts me. "That's not why I brought you here, you know?" I turn to look at him, even though I can barely make out his features in the dark night. It's cloudy, blocking almost all the moon tonight. "Not to talk."

I swear I see a hint of a smile there. "Well, I can't do anything other than talk, so we might as well."

I cock my head to the side, trying to make out his facial expression to see if he's messing with me, but I've got nothing. "Seriously?"

"Seriously," he says all too firmly. Damn it. I guess we aren't going to kiss anymore.

Fine. That's totally fine because I'm pretty sure the memory of that one fleeting kiss will be in my mind for the rest of my life. Pathetic? Maybe, but who the hell cares? It was by far the best kiss of my life.

And while I want more, maybe talking with Professor Barlowe won't be so bad. "My parents tried, I think, but I was a surprise. They didn't really want kids, at least that's the story I was told."

"You didn't know them?"

I shrug somberly as I take a deep breath. "I know them. I actually saw my dad not that long before I was adopted. They—well, he—tried to get me back a few times. I think he felt guilty, but he just couldn't get it together. I always wound up back in foster care."

I see the outline of him nodding along. "Drugs?" he asks, and I can tell it was hard for him to ask that question.

"Alcoholics, actually. Never touched the hard stuff." I try to laugh it off, but the memory of seeing my mom passed out on the couch all too damn often comes right up and clobbers me. It isn't funny. Her addiction wasn't funny. Neither was my father's. It was sad. Truly sad.

"I'm sorry," he says softly.

"They just didn't really handle life. Didn't want to be on a schedule, which having kids requires. My dad made more on the night shift, so that's what he wanted to work. But that meant my mom had to wake up early and get me to school, which never fucking worked out. I missed so much when I lived with them, though it's not like foster care was better."

He's quiet. Far too damn quiet, and I'm worried he might pity me now. I don't want that. Pity. It makes me sick to think about it. That's why I put on the show. I can stand people thinking I'm just like everyone else. Entitled. Or rich. That's fine. But different, sad, pathetic?

Yeah. I can't handle that.

"But it's okay. Blair came along and rescued my ass when I was almost thirteen, and I really am a rich spoiled kid now." I laugh slightly. "She wouldn't have it any other way."

"She sounds nice."

I grin. "She is. She was totally in love with Rhys and kind of chasing him when Bree literally ran right into Rhys's tattoo shop, hiding from her asshole foster father."

"Bree?"

"My sister." I laugh. "Well, I don't have any actual siblings, but Bree and Rhett, we met in foster care. They *became* my siblings."

"You looked out for each other," he murmurs.

I nod and go on, "We did. Blair and Rhys were working on adopting Bree, and they let us hang out at their bigass house. I mean, this house was insane. Huge and clean. Furnished so nicely. Lots of food. It was like a dream. And Rhett and I . . ."—I let out a deep breath —"God, we were so relieved for Bree."

I'll never forget how I felt when I knew she was going to be taken care of. That we didn't need to worry about Bree. That one of us was safe.

"What about you?" he asks me, surprising me a little.

"I was still stuck in foster hell, and so was Rhett, but after school we went to hang out with Bree. It was great." That familiar chill settles through me, and my eyes involuntarily close. "It all changed when Rhett and Bree were hanging out, and they couldn't reach me.

My asshole foster father went on a bender and beat the shit out of me."

I feel his entire body stiffen. "He hit you?"

I try to hold back the laugh because it's not funny, but his surprise is what I would expect from anyone who had a normal life. And once again, I worry that if I don't shut up, he's just going to end up pitying me. But I can't seem to shut my damn mouth. "It didn't happen that much. Just when he would get drunk, and he was pissed off because I forgot to take the trash out."

"Oh, yeah. That's a great reason to beat on a twelve-year-old kid," he bites out, and I hear the unchecked anger in his voice.

I put my hand out and rest it on his firm shoulder, oddly needing to comfort him. "I was okay, but when Blair and Rhys saw me, they freaked. They ended up getting custody of Rhett and me, and the rest is history."

"So that kid throwing a fit . . ."

I cringe, thinking about my super embarrassing moment in the coffee shop but not wanting to brush past it either. "I went back to that moment. Moments. When I was just a helpless kid," I barely breathe out. "I really don't want to talk anymore."

I can feel his body near mine. I can smell his expensive aftershave, and God, do I want to kiss him again. His lips are so damn full and soft. His hair is also really damn soft, despite holding its style so well. I thought for sure he had lots of gel or something in it, but nope. It's just perfect.

Everything about him is so damn put together and perfect, but the way he kisses? There was frenzied passion in that kiss I've never felt before and never expected. I want more. So much more.

"We could talk about you . . ." I say, instead of trying to kiss him again. I'm trying to behave here.

"No," he says instantly, but there's a hint of lightness there. It wasn't a quick *no*, not just shutting me down and rejecting me like I'm used to from him. "We should go back."

"Or we could kiss again," I blurt, and okay, so I didn't behave very long, but I tried.

"We really can't." But I hear the disappointment there. He wants to. He so wants to. "It's not a good idea, Fletcher."

I smile. *Fletcher.* I really like when he uses my first name instead of calling me *Mr. Moore.* So much less stuffy. "Because I'm a student in the fall, and you're a professor at the college I'm going to." I say it, hoping he understands just how dumb that sounds.

"Yes."

"I'm not enrolled right now. It's summer. Right now, I'm not a student," I say, trying to sound more confident than I actually feel.

"Fletcher . . ." There's that lightness again.

"It's a summer loophole. We could have three months of absolute bliss. Think about it."

He climbs off the rock and then holds out a hand for me. I take it, and for a moment I think he's going to kiss me again, but he just leans into me, his voice in my ear. "I can't."

And then he walks back to my Jeep and opens the door, climbing inside.

Can't.

Not doesn't want to—but can't.

I smile to myself as I walk to my Jeep and start it up to drive us back to campus.

I can work with that.

RONAN

I can't stop thinking about Fletcher. This is a real problem. It's been three days since we kissed and he took me out to the lake and we talked.

And he mentioned a summer loophole.

God, how badly did I want to take him up on that. Just let go and go for it for once in my life. Do something without really thinking about it. But I can't do that. I won't let myself.

I worked too damn hard to throw it all away for a summer fling.

And that was exactly what he was offering.

Hearing his story was eye-opening and tragic, but it doesn't really change anything. It can't. He's a student. A student I need to stay away from.

But because fate loves to fuck with me, as soon as I get settled at my desk in my office, in walks Fletcher. Man, does he look good. Of course he does. He's built and strong. His arms are bare because he's wearing a tank top—bright blue today. It matches his eyes. And his charcoal shorts cling to his perfectly sculpted ass far too well.

"Fletcher, what are you doing here?" My voice has no edge to it whatsoever.

I expect him to flirt, maybe even bring up the summer loophole again. Could I resist it if he did? But then I see Annie walking in right behind him, and my entire demeanor freezes.

Of course he's here helping the professor he'll be assisting next semester. Because he's a damn student, and that's why he's on campus.

Fuck. Me.

"Hey there, Professor," he says with a flirty smirk, but my smile has faded into a stern glare. Doesn't bother Fletcher in the slightest. "I'm here to help Professor Briggs."

"It's summer," I say in Annie's direction.

She doesn't seem bothered at all by my salty tone. She just waves me off. "We're done now, actually."

Fletcher parks his ass on the corner of my desk, making himself right at home. "She has a couple of classes this summer, and I told her I'd help with anything she needed. Even though I'm not a student at the moment." His eyes hold mine, and his intention is clear.

He wants to make it very well known that he's not a student. But he is. No matter how he spins it.

"I'll be right back. I'm going to go grab my purse," Annie announces and leaves.

I immediately stand up and walk over in front of Fletcher, where he still remains perched on my desk. What would it be like to spin him around and take him right here. Right now. Slide into his warm heat. The grip would be unbelievable. I'd never come back from it. There's no way I could. One kiss and I'm already addicted to the thought of having him.

"Professor?" Fletcher breaks through my dirty fantasy, his eyes glistening with mirth. He knows what I was thinking about. Heat creeps up my neck, and I do everything I can to push it away.

That would end my career.

As it should.

That won't be happening.

"You shouldn't be here," I try, forcing my thoughts away from fucking him over my desk toward the sickening thought of being caught. That isn't exciting for me. That would be devastating.

"It's really not a big deal."

"It is, Fletcher," I argue.

But he just stands up to his full height now, his body emanating heat. "I really like the way you say my name," he purrs, and damn it, I lean into him. Not close enough to touch, but it doesn't matter, I'm pulled to him all the same.

"Whoops." I hear Annie's voice, and I jerk back quickly, my gaze whipping over to her. She looks flustered but not upset. Not like she just walked in on one of her best friends—a professor, just like her—almost kissing a student.

Again.

"Did I interrupt something?" she asks, studying us closely, but she looks almost amused.

"No," I say quickly.

She smiles at me, it's a cocky sort of grin I don't love, and then she looks over at Fletcher. "You ready to go?'

"Go?" I ask.

She nods her head easily, slipping her purse on across her chest. "Yeah. I told him I'd buy him a burger at our favorite place."

"Our favorite place is a bar," I say stupidly, and she just continues to grin.

"It is."

"He's not twenty-one," I say, and just the words unsettle something deep inside me. Eighteen. He's eighteen years old. *Shit.*

"That's okay," Annie says, waving Fletcher on to follow her. "He can have a Coke with his burger. Come on. Nathan is meeting us there."

"Annie," I say but have absolutely no idea of what to say.

Fletcher doesn't really give me a chance though. "Don't worry, Professor," he says far too easily. "It'll be just a little bit of summer fun."

I could kill him.

I really could.

He knows exactly what he's doing. But he just walks right behind Annie, all innocent-like when I glare at him.

Not a damn care in the world.

And why should he? He's young and having a good time, as he should. He deserves that. I know that now. I've thought so damn much about it over the past few days. His constant need to always be on. To put on a show. That air of arrogance he works so hard to portray. It's clear now, it's an act. One carefully orchestrated so no one sees below the surface. He doesn't want anyone to know just how deeply the pain runs. And I want that so badly for him.

But he's not the one with so much to lose.

I can't just have fun.

I can't.

FLETCHER

O kay, so he's clearly not happy I'm here. But I couldn't resist. When Professor Briggs invited me along, I just couldn't say no.

"So Professor Barlowe, are you having a good summer?" I ask him, trying to make it sound innocent, but really my mind is back at his office. Me on his desk. What if I would have kissed him? Would he have pushed me away right away, or would he been just as helpless as I feel when it comes to this thing between us?

God, I wanted him to kiss me and never stop. I would have stripped naked and bent over his desk so damn fast, if I thought that's what he wanted too. But for now, I'm just playing the slow game.

Being cordial and hanging out near him. Totally normal behavior, I'm almost positive.

But he's glaring at me again.

"Oh my God, call him Ronan before that little vein in his forehead pops," Professor Briggs says with a laugh and places her hand over the middle of her chest. "And you can call me Annie." Then she points to Professor Harmon. "And him Nathan."

"Annie," I say with a smile and then nod. "I do like that." I turn to the professor who really does look like he's going to pop a vein. "Ronan."

"And Nathan," Professor Harmon finishes.

Ronan grumbles something into the beer he's drinking with his hamburger, but I don't think I want to hear that, so I let it go.

"So how is helping Annie, Fletcher?" Nathan asks, not making his friend answer my question, and I suppose that's for the best too.

"Pretty great. I think I could really get used to sociology."

Annie whoops, and Nathan just shakes his head at me. "Not math? Come on. What makes more sense than math?" he teases.

I laugh at that. "Yeah, no offense, but math is just about as entertaining as economics."

Annie chuckles. "See, you number boys will never understand. People will always trump numbers."

"Numbers never lie," Nathan says matter-of-factly.

"So this is what professors talk about in their free time?" I ask, and Annie cackles. Apparently, it is. But it's cool to see Ronan like this. He may be trying to keep his face serious, but I see the cracks in it when Annie teases him.

Or when Nathan teases Annie back for him. When they talk about the nightmare of grading and how they really do need to enjoy their summer now because they aren't really looking forward to the fall.

Not just yet.

But I can tell they all love their jobs.

We finish our burgers, and then Nathan asks Ronan to play pool. Ronan waves him off, as does Annie, but I don't. "I'm up for a game." I hop up, and Nathan looks excited.

"Thank God. Someone who knows how to have fun."

"Well, he *is* a damn fetus," Ronan grumbles. I raise my eyebrows in his direction.

"A fetus? Really?"

He looks away, and I swear I actually see a blush on his cheeks, but I can't be sure. Nathan just laughs at that. "Aw, Ronan. Are you sad you aren't the youngest anymore? Because you're pretty damn close to fetus stage."

Ronan surprises me when he raises his middle finger in his friend's direction, but Nathan doesn't seem surprised. It's wild to see him almost free like this.

Could he ever be like this with me?

I head over to the pool table and start a game with Nathan, but the whole time, my eyes keep drifting to Ronan. God, I'm even obsessed with his name.

If Nathan notices, he doesn't call me on it, and I'm grateful because I don't think Ronan would like that at all, and I'm trying to get on his good side, damn it.

That kiss.

That kiss is ingrained in my brain. Just planted right there in my memory, and I play it over and over again.

I want to kiss him again. So damn badly.

Fetus.

I'm not a damn fetus. I may only be eighteen, and I may act like a shithead, but I'm very mature for my age. I had to grow up young, and I can handle hanging out with people ten years, or even more, older than me.

And Ronan—I don't think he's even ten years older than me. I should do some research and find out his exact age. He looks really young for a professor. I don't think he's even hit his thirties yet.

"How old are you, Nathan?" I ask, trying like hell to sound casual but failing and failing hard because way to just blurt that out, Fletcher.

"Thirty-nine. Why?" he asks cautiously.

I shrug, lining up a shot and sending the number four ball to the corner pocket. "Just curious. Since you all called me a *fetus.*"

He tosses his head back and laughs at that. I miss the next shot, and he lines up to take the next one. "Well, that's what we call Ronan. Annie's turned thirty-five six times since I met her." That makes me smile. "And then there's Ronan, who just turned twenty-six."

Twenty-six.

I can't fight the smile on my face at that because *I knew it.* He's not that much older than me.

I can also work with that.

63

RONAN

No. *I refuse to believe he's here. Right outside my house.*
        Shirtless too, I might add.

Good God, his body is just stupid. I mean, stupid fucking hot. He's
nothing but muscle. Sculpted, chiseled muscle that's so damn defined
I can follow each line, which I do with my eyes as I stand outside my
front door and ogle the hell out of him.

He has on a pair of loose black shorts and has earbuds in his ears,
smiling as he runs up to me, taking them out of his ears. He's sweaty,
and his hair is matted, which makes me think he's been running for a
bit, but he doesn't seem winded at all.

I'm also wearing shorts, a t-shirt and Nikes for my morning jog.
All perfectly in place. I was ready for a nice, relaxing run, and now
here Fletcher is, just barreling into my life.

I'm not nearly strong enough for this. "Are you stalking me?" My
tone is nowhere near as irritated as I want it to be.

And he must notice because he's grinning by the time he stops in
front of me. "Nope. Happy accident." He looks behind me at my
house—it's a modest but modern and well-kept, two-bedroom, two-
bath, only a couple of blocks from campus. "This is where you live,
huh?"

This isn't good. "Oh God, now you're really going to start stalking me, aren't you?"

He waggles his brows at me playfully. "Quite possibly."

I actually frown at that, though, realizing how ill-timed my joke is. The Rhonda Tuttle situation is still mainstream news. Still a huge deal around here, and here I am making a joke about it, while flirting with a damn student.

"Right. Well, don't do that, and have a nice run," I say, brushing past him. I can do this. I can and will resist him. It's not appropriate. What if someone sees him outside my house?

I start to jog down the street, but of course, Fletcher is right there with me, running alongside me with a smile on his handsome face.

"Fletcher, surely this isn't your regular route," I try.

"Actually, it is." He keeps up with me easily as we round a corner. "I can't believe I've been jogging past your house all year, and I didn't even know it."

"You know, if people see us together . . ."

"What people?" he asks, and I don't think he's just messing with me. I think he actually wants to know what I'm worried about.

I liked him better when he was just an arrogant shithead.

Okay, not really.

"Like people who could fire me," I say with no hint of joking in my voice because it's simply not funny. It could very well happen.

"They'd fire you for running?" he asks, and I can't tell if he's messing with me or not, so I stop my jog and face him.

"Fletcher."

He stops running too and cocks his head to the side innocently, but I don't really buy it. "I'm serious." He laughs, which tells me he isn't really. "They aren't going to fire you for running next to me."

"They could. I'm a professor at the college. You are a student."

"Not a student," he quickly corrects, and I groan, leaning my head back and looking up at the sky, I guess for strength or something. But the clouds and the sun give me nothing.

"Whatever. Let's just run," I concede because there's really no arguing with Fletcher.

He shrugs it off easily, and we take off again. It's a brisk run, and it feels good. All my muscles ache, and my chest puffs with air as I breathe through it, but there's a runner's high like none other pumping through my veins by the time we circle back to my house.

We're both out of breath and sweaty when we reach the sidewalk in front of my house. We both stop and stare at the door, then Fletcher looks at me with those big hopeful eyes. "You know, the polite thing to do would be to invite me in for some water."

He doesn't want water.

We both know it.

We'd be going in for one thing and one damn thing only. It's crossing a line. One I shouldn't. One I really can't.

At least, if I'm smart.

But I feel nothing but stupid when I nod my head slowly and motion for him to follow me, my heart racing for a whole new reason and my throat so dry with anticipation, I can't form actual words.

We go into my house, and I lock the door as if someone might follow us. It's insane. It's so damn quiet on my block most of the time, but especially in summer. We didn't pass anyone when we were on our run, but that doesn't mean the paranoia isn't there, which should tell me how wrong this is. But I can't say no.

I can't deny myself this moment with him, and I don't know why.

All I know for certain is I haven't wanted to kiss someone so damn badly before in my life, but I do resist that. Thank fuck.

I walk into my kitchen and pull open the fridge, pulling out two bottles of water and handing one of them to him when he joins me. "This place is nice."

I look around at the sparsely decorated home with wood floors. It is nice. I love it here. And I invited a student into it. My home.

"This is a bad idea," I say carefully.

Fletcher seems to ignore that completely, though, unscrewing the cap on the bottle of water and downing damn near half of it. I try not to watch the way his throat flexes each time he swallows, and I open my own bottle, taking a large gulp.

"Fletcher . . ." I try again, but he just places his bottle of water on the counter and walks closer to me. My heart stutters in my chest. He's so damn beautiful, I swear it hurts.

"Why?" He stops in front of me, the tip of his tennis shoes touching mine as he reaches for my bottle of water and takes it from me, placing it next to his.

"Why is it a bad idea that you're in my house right now?" I ask, astonished that he'd even need to ask. But I know it's more for my benefit. "You know why," I barely manage to say.

His hand trails down the middle of my shirt, my sweat making the fabric stick against my skin, but he doesn't seem to mind in the slightest. "I can't stop thinking about you." His eyes flick up to mine. "About that kiss."

"The kiss that shouldn't have happened," I say, wrapping my hand around his wrist and halting his movement.

"Because you didn't enjoy it?"

"No," I answer instantly. No point in lying.

"Because you pity me and my sad as hell story?" This question was harder for him to ask me. I can tell by the nervous look on his face, like he's afraid that's actually why I kissed him.

I reach one hand up, brushing it over his cheek before I cup his face in my hand and look him dead in the eyes. "No," I say firmly.

He looks relieved, and it breaks my heart. "Then why?"

"You know why, Fletcher." I'm still holding onto his wrist. His finger is resting between my pecs. "I'm a professor, and you're a student. Summer loophole or not."

"But it is summer, and I'm not a student. I'm not your student." He sounds as frustrated as I feel, and goddammit, I want to give in. He's technically right, I know that.

"Have you seen the news lately?"

He huffs at that and pulls out of my grip. I let his hand go, but he doesn't move away from me other than that. "What, that professor who was fucking her student?"

I nod. So he has heard. "Yes."

"Of course I've seen it. It's literally everywhere."

He's not wrong. Every time you turn on the television, it seems like this story is running, and our university is on blast. "Then how do you not understand that we cannot do this?"

He looks truly perplexed now as he looks at me. "Because it's not the same thing."

"It is," I argue. "At it's very basic roots, it is, and you know it."

"Look, Professor," He starts, his tone having a very distinctive edge to it. "That was different. For one, she was twice his age."

"I'm still much older than you."

He scoffs at that. "Only eight damn years. Seven and a half, actually. That's nothing. Eighteen is fully damn grown when you grow up the way I did." I flinch at that but let him continue. "I know you see me as an immature fuckup—"

"I don't." I feel the need to interrupt him, to correct him immediately, because the truth is maybe I did see him that way before, but I don't now.

"Good. Because I'm not," he says very clearly. "That kid . . ." I know he's talking about the student on the news. "He is. I've seen interviews with him. It's like nothing bad has ever happened to him his entire life, probably hadn't."

"What does that matter?" I try.

"Because I'm sure that was traumatic for him. He's out on his own. His hot college professor, who's twice his age, seduces him and then tosses him away like that? Of course he's fucked up from it."

"I have nothing to offer you, Fletcher. That would be us. You're out on your own now, and I'm a professor."

He holds up a hand to silence me, and damn it, it works. I'm quiet as I listen to him. He holds up one finger. "One, it's not my first time on my own, not by a long shot. I was on my own for most of my childhood, and it forced me to grow up really damn fast." I don't bother opening my mouth again when he holds up a second finger. "Two, you didn't seduce me. I've read and listened to the interviews, she seduced the hell out of him. She manipulated him and used her power when he first resisted to get what she wanted."

"Exactly. That's the problem with professor/student relationships, Fletcher. No one in a position of power should ever start a relationship with someone who is so vulnerable."

He steps into me, his mouth so damn close, I'm transfixed, even before his lips start moving as he talks. "And who exactly has the power here? Huh?" He doesn't let me try to answer. "He was still in her class when they started fucking, and he was struggling. Even she admits that. She held grades over his head. He was here on a scholarship, and he needed that damn grade. I understand why that was wrong, but you and me?" He motions between the small amount of space between our bodies. "No power struggle whatsoever."

"Fletcher," I breathe, hating how much sense he's making, but it has to be because he's standing so close and making me so damn horny, I can barely think. His erection brushes against mine, and I groan softly, wanting to give in so damn bad.

"Ronan, it's not the same," he says, using my name. There's no hint of teasing, and I hear the desperate plea in his voice. The same desperation I feel to not have to follow the rules just once. "I'm not in your class. I don't plan to be in your class ever again, but even when I was, I was the top of my class. I didn't need a bump up, and I'm not on a scholarship. Hell, if anything happened, and I was in danger of getting kicked out of school, I really wouldn't put it past my mom to buy the whole place just to keep me here." I let a surprised laugh slip from my mouth, and he looks momentarily surprised as well by my laughter, but grins. "She's not that rich, but her dad is, and you know when he kicks it, it's all going to her."

"Jesus, Fletcher." I laugh again.

He wraps a hand around the back of my neck, pulling me into him, but he doesn't kiss me. His forehead rests against mine. "It's not the same thing."

"I can't lose my job, Fletcher." My throat is raw with the honesty. "It's everything to me. I worked hard to get here."

"You won't," he whispers, and damn it, in that moment, I believe him. I believe it could all be okay. "Take a shower with me."

All I can do is nod in agreement. There's no denying how badly we both want this, and even if I regret it later, I'm going to let myself have it.

At least for now.

FLETCHER

oly fuck. He said yes. I don't waste any time either. I don't want him to overthink this. I mean yeah, I want to know he for sure wants it, but I can feel it deep in my bones he does.

I get why he's worried. I'm not an idiot. The news is all over this latest scandal, and honestly, that professor really did deserve to get fired. She held all the cards. She was in charge, not to mention she was married to another person.

Everything about that situation is icky as hell, but this isn't that, and I'll spend every free second I have proving that to Ronan, if he'll just let me. I was shocked as all hell to see him walking out of a house near campus on my run today, but then I just sort of accepted it as fate being on my side.

I'm okay with that too. Last time fate stepped in, I finally got a real family. This time, I get Ronan.

At least, for the summer.

I try not to let that last thought sour my mood as I pull him toward a hallway I'm assuming will lead us to a bathroom. I don't really care where we end up though. Drenched in sweat is just fine by me, as long as there's touching. Lots and lots of touching.

And kissing. God, let there be more kissing.

"All the way to the end," his voice rumbles in my ear as he holds onto my hand and follows me. A thrill goes through my entire body. Ronan is totally on board. This is happening.

I make it to the bedroom at the end of the hall and notice a neatly made bed in the middle and a bathroom with an open door across the room. I grin and pull him that way. I hear his light chuckle at my enthusiasm, but I can't be bothered.

I'm finally going to have him naked. Wet and naked. Hell yes.

I go straight into the bathroom and flip on the light, heading for the shower and turning it on, just making myself right at home. My brain is too jumbled with excitement to care. When I turn around to face Ronan, though, I nearly choke on the saliva pooling in my mouth.

He's removed his t-shirt, showing off his trim torso with just the lightest dusting over his firm pecs. He's maybe not as defined as me—thanks to a gym in my building and spending a lot of time there—but the man is cut. "Holy fuck."

He gives me a slow, teasing grin as his fingers hook into the waistband of his shorts. Shorts, might I add, that are deliciously tented with his arousal. Fuck. Yes.

"Please," I whimper. I don't care how pathetic I sound. I've been dreaming of this damn moment, and it's here.

I watch as he slips out of his shoes, his fingers still on his waistband. "Shirt." He nods in my direction.

"Abso-fucking-lutley," I say, having zero qualms about getting naked. I whip my shirt off over my head and toss it to the ground.

He chuckles again at my desperation, and I don't move my eyes from him as I take my shoes off quickly. He slides his shorts and underwear down, freeing his hard, veiny cock that jumps up and slaps against his stomach. My mouth waters as I take him all in.

"Damn, you have a nice dick," I say dumbly as he removes his shorts and briefs, along with his socks before kicking the pile away.

He moves closer to me, totally naked, his hard, solid body moving gracefully across the marble bathroom floor. "Let me see yours."

I waste no time shoving my shorts and underwear down and off. Removing my socks and leaving me totally naked before him far more quickly than he did, but I'm not interested in teasing. I want to get to the kissing and the touching.

I move my eyes down to where his dick is standing tall, my cock hard as hell and straining in his direction. I notice the bead of pre-cum on the flared head, and before I can think too hard about it, I'm wrapping my hand around his thick cock. He lets out a strangled moan and thrusts into my hand. "Fuck."

"If you want to. I'm up for anything," I tease as I lean forward, his cock still in my hand, and press my lips against his. I stroke him slowly, and he only waits for the briefest moment before he's kissing me hard.

It has the exact same amount of frantic passion as our first kiss, and I relish in the way his dick jerks in my hand as my tongue sweeps inside his mouth to taste him. We kiss as I stroke his hard length, and he directs us toward the shower. He opens the glass door, and we don't separate for even a second as we climb inside and under the hot water.

His luscious lips are pressed against mine as I stroke him, and the hot water hits the back of my neck, sliding down my already heated body. His hands move to my back, sliding over each muscle there as we kiss. When his big hands grip my ass, I groan and thrust forward. My cock bumps against his and makes me moan into his mouth.

"You're way too hot," he says against my mouth, nipping and biting down over my jaw and neck as I fist his cock, my own dick leaking and begging for relief, but I'm not ready for that yet.

Now that we're kissing again, I don't want it to stop. I don't want this to be over. "So are you. Stupid hot for such an old man," I tease, and he nips my bottom lip with his teeth.

I yelp but groan as I grip him harder, and his tongue swipes over the spot he bit. His hand slides down my crease, teasing me, but not going near my hole where I want him the most. I want to beg him, but I hold out.

His hands move back up over my ass and my back, up to my shoulders as he kisses me, then moves a hand down to the wrist of my hand still stroking him. He gently pushes it away, and I'm worried it's all over when he shocks the hell out of me by reaching for my cock and sliding his against it, stroking us both in his big hand.

He can't wrap it all the way around, but there's enough friction there to send my eyes rolling into the back of my head. Nothing has ever felt this damn good, and I tell him so as I grip his wet hair and we kiss. I want to keep him here in this moment. Never let him go.

The head of his cock grazes the sensitive ridge of mine, and we both gasp, our hips moving together in tandem as we race toward release because there's no stopping it now. We're both too close to slow it down.

It's too damn much, and when I feel that familiar tingle start to race down my back, I shout out in surprise, ripping my mouth from his just as my cum spurts all over his cock and lower stomach. He cries out a moment later, still stroking us both, and his cum hits my nearly spent dick, causing more cum to dribble from my tip. He strokes us both gently, wringing us out until we both become too sensitive.

We stare at each other. Both of us breathless and sated before his mouth crashes against mine, and we get lost in another heated kiss. It's like we can't get enough. The water starts to cool, and our kisses start to slow, but I don't want to let him go.

"How about we get some lunch?" he asks, and oh my God, he's not kicking me out. I nod my head, but I kiss him some more, unable to keep my lips off him. I nip and lick at his lips and a slow smile moves over his mouth. "Fletcher?"

"Oh, right," I say, realizing my fingers are tangled in his hair. "Lunch."

"First, let's clean off." He kisses my lips, then moves away from me a little bit. I miss his body instantly, but then he grabs some body wash and lathers it in his hands before moving his hands to my chest and sliding them all over me.

I tip my head back on a soft moan as he cleans me. I can't seem to do anything else. I never want him to stop touching me. He quickly cleans himself and then grabs the shampoo and shocks the hell out of me when he washes my hair, his fingers like heaven on my scalp.

My eyes fall closed as I just feel—his fingers in my hair, him directing me under the water to rinse off. His body guides mine out of the stream of the water, so he can clean himself, and then his mouth is back on mine in a sweet, devastating kiss because I've never been cared for like that in my life.

And I could easily become addicted to it.

But he turns off the water, and we dry off before he wraps the towel around his trim waist. Holy shit, the guy is gorgeous. I knew he would be. He's lean, no fat on him like I suspected, but a little more muscle than I expected.

"I'll be right back," he says, and I nod dumbly as he leaves the bathroom. I watch the way the white towel clings to his absolutely delectable ass as he leaves.

He comes back with a t-shirt and a pair of sweats for me and a set for himself too. While I'd rather remain naked, I relent and get dressed before we go out into his living room.

"You okay with sandwiches?" he asks me, and again I nod my head dumbly. I can't seem to speak—which, let me tell you, is kind of new for me.

But I'm suddenly afraid to say or do the wrong thing. That was . . . that was just *wow*, and I want to do it again.

"Are you okay?" he asks me, coming closer and grasping my jaw in one of his big hands. "Fletcher, talk to me."

"That was amazing," I blurt out, and a cautious smile forms on his face.

"It was, but if you're having second thoughts—"

"Never," I say quickly. "Oh God, no. No second thoughts. I want to do it again. And again. I want to do more. So much more."

I swear I see a quick flush on his cheeks, but I can't be sure. "Are you sure? It's . . ."

"Perfect. More than I could have ever imagined," I say quickly because the last thing I want for him to think is that I didn't absolutely love what we did. "I'm just afraid of fucking it up," I say honestly.

His smile fades, replaced by something sadder. "It can't last, Fletcher. If we do this, you have to know exactly where we stand. We

75

have to be on the same page, and we need to communicate. I don't want to hurt you, but I can't . . ." He swallows hard and stops speaking, but I already know. I let that process for a moment.

"I know, and I understand. Your job is important to you." He nods his head slowly. "And that's okay with me." I force a smile. "Summer loophole, right?"

He studies me closely for a moment and then gives a curt nod. "Summer. Yes."

Something twists deep inside me, telling me to run and not be an idiot, but I can't say no to this.

Our time being limited or not, it doesn't matter.

I'll take this chance to have him. Even if it's only for a little while.

RONAN

The summer loophole.

This is *so* not smart. But I couldn't say no. My God, I did so much more than kiss him this time, and I can't regret it. His body is ridiculous.

I knew it was, but seeing him naked and actually getting to touch him? Yeah, that was a whole new level.

And I can't bring myself to regret it. We ordered sandwiches, and now he's searching through my Netflix for something to watch as we sit on my couch. His thigh is touching mine, and I feel his warmth through the material of both of our sweats.

"Oh yes! Murder doc!"

"What?" I ask, turning my head to look at him instead of the screen.

"Murder docs are my fave. I could binge-watch them all damn day."

"Should I be worried?" I ask, a smile on my lips. "You're awfully excited to watch a documentary about someone who was murdered."

"Lots of someones," he says, bright excitement in his voice, but then his eyes meet mine with a hint of vulnerability in them. "I mean, is this okay? We can watch something else."

I chuckle at that and look back at the screen. "Start it up."

"Yes," he whoops and starts it, putting the remote on the coffee table and digging into his meatball sub. "And no, you don't need to worry," he says around a full bite.

I chuckle at that too and hand him a napkin. He takes it, wiping at his mouth.

"I just think it's fascinating, you know? What people can do to each other. How wrong it can all go. It's crazy."

"Yeah, I guess I like a good murder doc too, here and there."

I see a cute blush on his cheeks, but he just goes back to enjoying his sandwich. I like seeing this side of him.

"You know, I don't remember you ever being that fascinated by economics."

He laughs at that, swallowing an extra-large bite. "Sorry, Professor, but like I said . . . boring as fuck."

I feign hurt, and he laughs at that, his embarrassment seeming to fade away. The much more confident Fletcher back. "Now, sociology . . ."

"Stop, or I'll never touch your dick again," I joke because yeah . . . he could read a sociology textbook out loud right now, and I'd gladly touch his dick.

He mimes zipping his lips at that, his eyes going wide. "I'll never say another word about sociology."

I chuckle and then playfully shove his heavy arm. "I'm trying to watch this," I tease, looking back at the screen, but I can feel Fletcher's eyes on me. I slowly turn to look at him. "What's wrong?"

A shy smile slides over his lips. "You're just . . ." I wait. "You're different. Lighter. You're like actually joking with me."

I think about that for a moment. "Is that a bad thing?"

"No," he says instantly. "I like it." His smile makes me smile. Damn thing is contagious.

"Good. I like it too," I say and then I lean over and steal his lips in a soft kiss. One that lingers there for a while because I don't want to pull away, and he doesn't seem to be in much of a hurry either.

I do feel different when I'm around him. It's a strange thing. I get what he's saying when he was talking about growing up fast. I had to grow up really damn fast too. I put so much on the back burner, and when I'm with him, there's a lightness to my soul.

The kiss quickly turns heated though, our food forgotten as he tears his shirt off over his head and then instantly goes for mine. I help him remove the fabric from my body and pull his larger one on top of me as I fall back on the couch.

It's a tight fit, but we make it work. His hand slides into my sweats, and I'm really damn glad I went without underwear because his deep, sultry groan fills my ears as he kisses me harder as he starts to stroke me.

"Fuck, Ronan," he breathes. "I don't think I'll ever get enough."

"Summer," I gasp because I need to remind him—and myself—that this is only for summer. It will only work if we keep that in mind.

I can feel him smile against my lips as he trails kisses from my jaw and down my neck, his tongue peeking out and licking my nipple as he moves down my body. "Right. Summer." He licks the other nipple, making it pebble with intense need. My fingers grip his hair as he moves lower and lower down my stomach. "We have the whole summer for me to explore this insane body you've been hiding."

"Not hiding," I gasp as his lips meet the waistband of my sweats that are tented by my rock-hard erection. He moves his hands to the waistband, slowly lowering them. Teasing us both. The tip of my cock escapes, but he doesn't pull them any lower. No, Fletcher might actually kill me this way because his tongue flicks over the sensitive tip, playing with me.

He drags the flat of his tongue through my slit, moaning heavily. "Oh, fuck me. You taste good."

I groan, my fingers digging into his hair, my cock leaking like crazy. "Please."

"Oh." His large blue eyes flick up to me, his tongue resting on the tip of my cock. "You're begging now?"

"Yes," I gasp, not caring at all. "Please."

He runs his tongue over the tip again, his gaze devilish as he looks up at me. "Please what?"

My breathing is rapid as I stare down at him, his big eyes, his plush lips, his pink tongue driving me wild. "Please suck me, Fletcher. I need it."

"Oh, fuck yes," he says just as he pushes my sweats down further and fully engulfs me in the hot wet heat of his mouth.

"Oh God," I moan, my fingers gripping his soft strands. I unintentionally buck my hips upward, and while it makes him gag slightly, my dick hitting the back of his throat, it doesn't seem to deter him in the slightest.

He sucks me harder, one of his hands moving to my balls, rolling them and tugging lightly, driving me completely insane. I'm a mumbling mess, putty in his hands when I realize his other hand is pushed into his own sweats, working vigorously as his hips thrust forward.

"Fuck, that feels good." I say, tipping my head back and getting lost in the intense suction.

I can feel him smiling around my shaft, his mouth totally full. My cock slams into his mouth, and he doesn't let up. He just keeps going, sucking me so damn hard, I cry out. "I'm going to come," I warn him, but his hand on his own dick only moves faster as he sucks me harder.

My cum floods his mouth at the same time he moans loudly, both our bodies going taut with pleasure. My cock nearly pulls all the way out of his mouth as spurt after spurt hits his tongue, his mouth open and waiting.

I can see the corded muscles of his neck pulled tight as he swallows my load and removes his hand from his sweats. When we're both wrung dry, he lays his head down on my thighs, wrapping his arms around my legs.

I don't mind the mess, the sticky hand on my thighs. I can't move.

"I think you killed me," I breathe.

He chuckles but doesn't say a word, just remains in the same spot for a while before he looks up at me again with a boyish grin. "You know, we probably should have had the whole safe sex talk before. My mom would kill me."

I cringe at that thought because yeah, we should have. "I got tested three months ago and haven't been with anyone for . . ." I cringe yet again, thinking about just how long it's been. "A while."

Thankfully, he doesn't ask how long. "I was tested a month ago and six months before that. All negative."

I nod, but for some reason, I wasn't concerned. Not at all. I trust him.

Jesus, when was the last time I fully trusted someone like that, and how the hell did we get here?

"Cool. So unlimited cum then?" He grins at me, lifting his head and waggling his eyebrows.

I can't help the bark of laughter that leaves my mouth. "I suppose so." But the moment is too heavy, with the trust thoughts in my head, and panic sets in. I open my mouth to remind him that it's only for the summer when he sits up, stopping me by lifting his hand in the air.

"Unlimited cum for the summer only. I know."

My gut sinks at the thought, but I nod my head anyway. This is important. It's the responsible thing to do. Keep that in our heads.

"Why don't we go shower again, since you got me all nice and dirty?" He grins, making the moment light again, and I could kiss him for doing that. And that's exactly what I do because I can.

Just for this summer.

FLETCHER

No offense to Rhett and Bree, but for the first time I can remember in a really long time, I really just want them to leave my place. And yes, I feel really guilty about that because I love them. *Obviously.*

But damn it, I could be getting naked with my very hot professor right now. But Bree and Rhett decided to surprise me this afternoon for an impromptu sibling hangout.

So instead of heading over to Ronan's place after his class today, I'm here watching cheesy horror movies and eating pizza with them.

"Jesus fuck! Run, you dumbass!" Bree shouts at the television, and okay, I smile because I really love her.

"Bree, it's kind of hard to run in heels like that, I'm sure," Rhett supplies as he takes a bite of pizza.

"I wouldn't know," she says, kicking her Converse tennis shoes up on my coffee table.

I grin and then look at Rhett. "Where the hell is your better half, by the way?"

Rhett looks sad but happy at the same time because he's totally whipped, and those two are together as often as possible. "Taking a summer class."

"Aw, do you miss him?" I tease, already knowing the answer.

"Fuck yes, I do. He'll be done in an hour, and then you can bet your asses I'm out of here." Is it bad that I'm happy to have that timeline? Yes, it is. I'm glad they stopped by. I really am. Bree is going off to New York in the fall.

An uncomfortable feeling sweeps over me at that thought. I don't think I've fully allowed myself to think about that before, and I sure don't want to think about it right now.

"Earth to Fletcher." I hear Bree and turn to look at her.

"What?"

She cocks her head to the side, studying me. "Oh my God, what are you thinking about? The hottie professor?"

Rhett grins, and I love and hate that they both know about that now. "No." But I also don't want to tell them about what I was really thinking about. How Bree is leaving and won't be in the same state for the first time since I met her.

"Yeah, right. Then why didn't you answer me," Rhett says suspiciously.

"Didn't hear you." I eye him. "What?"

"I asked when you're going to finally let me give you a tattoo, you big baby." He nudges my shoulder, and I laugh heartily at that.

"Never," I give him the same answer I always have, sweeping my hand over the length of my body. "You don't mess with perfection, Rhett. You know that."

He rolls his eyes at me, and Bree fake gags. It's a good time. "Fine. Then tell us more about your hot professor," he counters.

Yeah, that's not going to happen. I'm not sure why I haven't told them about the kiss—and uh, more—that's happened between Ronan and me, all I know is that I haven't. Which is kind of strange.

I know that it's just a summer fling—he goes out of his way to mention that as often as possible—as if I could forget. But I know it is, and normally, I'd give Rhett and Bree far too many details about my hookups just to watch them squirm uncomfortably and beg me to stop. But not with this.

For some reason, this seems off-limits.

"The professor who hates him." Bree so helpfully adds, and I should tell them that maybe he doesn't hate me all that much anymore. Maybe he doesn't hate me at all, but I don't. I'm silent.

They move on to a different topic easily though. Before I know it, they're heading out, and I'm jogging over to Ronan's house because I don't think driving and parking near his house would be a good idea.

It doesn't take me long to get there, and as soon as he opens the door to let me in, my lips are on his. The door is closed and secure behind us as we make our way to his bedroom, not wasting any time.

I mean, we only have the summer, right?

There really is no time to waste.

He doesn't seem to mind that I'm sweaty at all, his hands working to get rid of every scrap of my clothing as I work on his, our mouths tangled the entire time. I can't stop kissing him. I've never been this addicted to kissing in my life, but I don't want to stop.

We fall onto his bed, completely naked, our legs intertwined as we kiss, not really in a hurry, now that we're both naked.

"Hi," he breathes against my mouth as he softly kisses my lips.

"Hi," I say back, a stupid grin on my face as I kiss him back. He pushes me to my back, his hands going to my wrists as he lifts my arms above my hands and pins me there, straddling me. Our cocks are hard as he drags his heavy shaft over mine, making me groan.

I was here yesterday. I felt him like this and saw him like this just yesterday for the first time—but it doesn't matter—I'm already addicted. I already missed this in the time we were apart.

Yesterday, I was certain he would kick me out as soon as we finished cleaning up, but he didn't. He just gave me another set of clothes, and we went back to binge-watch Netflix until it was time to eat again.

After dinner, I thought maybe he'd need some space, so I was the one to initiate me leaving for the night. He walked me to the door, and with a sweet, yet still bone-melting kiss, he invited me back here today.

Which I happily accepted with an eager nod and another heated kiss before finally prying myself away. I know I need to keep my wits here. I know I need to protect my heart—I'm really not an idiot—but I can't seem to.

I want this. I want this so damn badly.

He uses one hand to pin both my wrists and then drags his free hand down the middle of my stomach, through the carefully sculpted abs I'm pretty damn proud of. "Your body is insane."

I grin at that, beaming up at him. "It likes you too."

He rolls his eyes at me, but there's a smile playing on his lips. Goddamn, he's beautiful. I've never seen anyone so beautiful when they smile. And I think it's because it's more rare with him.

His firm hand wraps around my cock, and I nearly bow off the bed. "Shit."

He grins again, and this time it's confident and sexy as all hell. "You're too perfect."

I thrust into his hand, my hands still held above my head as I tilt my head back and give into the pleasure he's offering me. He strokes me from base to tip, over and over, driving me wild. My hips buck into each stroke, and I'm a panting mess by the time his big dick joins the party, his hand wrapped around both of us as he thrusts against me.

Each stroke is a jolt to my system. Each one, I imagine he's driving inside my body. I want it so damn badly, but before I can beg him to fuck me, my balls pull up tight, close to my body, and I let loose, my cum spraying my stomach and chest. A moment later, he goes over too. His hand grips my wrists tight as we move languidly, milking our orgasms before he releases my wrists and collapses on top of me.

I drop my arms down and wrap them around him, feeling his muscled back, slick with sweat as we both work to come down from the high. He pulls back enough to place a soft kiss on my lips, then rolls off me and onto his back, both of us still panting.

"Have fun with your siblings today?" he asks.

I let out a surprised laugh. "I have our cum all over me. Last thing I want to talk about right now."

He chuckles and then rolls to his side. Apparently, he's not bothered by the mess, and I like that. Someone so damn orderly who doesn't seem to mind a little filth now and then. "I know you're close. I just wanted to know more about them," he says softly, and I think I'm shocked stupid.

I roll to my side now, facing him, but he isn't really looking at me directly. He wants to know more about me.

I try not to read too much into that, but I also can't deny him either. "We are close. It was good to see them. It's always really good to see them. They're kind of my home."

He nods his head slowly as if he understands. "They were in foster care too." It's something I already told him, so he's not really asking, but I hear his unspoken question.

"They were. I don't know why we just clicked, but we did. Obviously, we all knew a lot of kids like us, but it was us three from the moment we met."

He smiles at that, and I can't help but drag my thumb over his bottom lip, tracing the shape of it. "I'm glad you had them."

"Me too," I say with a happy smile as he grabs my wrist, but he doesn't pull me away. "I kind of felt bad today because all I wanted to do was come here and be with you. I almost kicked their asses out."

He chuckles, his whole face lighting up with it. "You did not."

"I did," I say with a bigass grin and lean into him, my lips pressing against his, his hand still around my wrist. "I think I'm a little addicted."

He smiles, but it's soft as he reaches up with his free hand and brushes the hair out of my eyes. "I think I may be too."

My heartbeat stutters at that, but he doesn't let me say anything else before kissing me hard. I don't waste any time kissing him back, but it doesn't become heated like before. It's sweet and sexy all at the same time.

"Why is your job so important again?" I ask, trying to joke, but really if it wasn't, would it have to end with summer? Could we have more of this?

He moves back away from me slowly, releasing me, but resting his hand on my naked hip as we lie facing each other.

"I mean, I know you love it," I say.

He offers a sad smile at that. "I do." His voice almost cracks, and I'm worried I ruined the mood completely, but he clears his throat and continues, "I need this job, Fletcher. I can't lose it."

I hear the shakiness in his voice. The fear there, and I know just how damn important this job is to him, even if I don't know why exactly. "I'll do everything I can to make sure that you won't." I lick my lips, then say firmly, "But I just want to know you better too."

He leans forward and captures my lips with his own, and somehow, I know I'm not getting that answer.

He's deflecting, but I let him because damn, what a tactic.
We'll talk later.

RONAN

"Oh fuck, this is insanely stupid. Fletcher, we can't do this." I gasp as he lowers to his knees. My ass is resting against my desk in my office, and I know we shouldn't do this. I know it, but I can't seem to tell him no.

Why?

I have no damn idea.

Okay, that's not true at all. It has to do with his smile. And those big blue eyes. And that cocky attitude I thought I hated but actually really like now. And the way he kisses. And his laugh.

Goddammit. This is not good.

It's been one week of fooling around every single day since the first, and I can't seem to get enough of him. "Relax." His hand moves to the button of my pants as he undoes it and the zipper, pulling my pants and underwear down in a sexy, confident move. "The door is locked. The shade on the window is pulled down, and it's summer," he purrs, his hand wrapping around my fully erect length as he looks up at me. "No one is here."

"Annie is here." I point out because that's the whole reason he was on campus today.

He rubs the tip of my cock over his full lips, making me pant as he looks up at me with those wide eyes. "Nope. She went home. It's just us."

This is a bad idea, but I can't and don't want to resist him. I nod my head, my fingers threading through his hair as he starts to take me into his warm mouth. "You're so damn good at that."

I love the feel of his smile around my cock as he works me. He strokes me in his hand as he takes the rest of my dick into his mouth. The suction, along with the firm grip, is enough to set my body on fire, my release already breaking toward the surface.

"I want you so damn bad. You're so beautiful, Fletcher," I say because this is something I can be honest about. I don't know why I haven't talked more about myself.

He's told me a lot about him. I know about his childhood that was less than stellar. I feel like I already know his entire adopted family now, including his little brothers, Max and Ian, because he's spoken about them.

We've fooled around a hell of a lot, but he's talked a lot too. And I've listened. But I haven't offered anything back. Nothing about my past. It's something I hold so damn closely. Something I don't like thinking about. So I push it away, but I owe him that. I know I do.

Even if this is just a summer thing, there's no denying we care about each other.

I nearly laugh at the thought. I never thought we'd be here in this moment—with this beautiful man on his knees for me. The slurping noises he's making as he sucks me off is obscene and only serving to push me that much closer to the edge.

"I'm close," I breathe, and as it usually does, that only makes him double down. Stroking me faster as he sucks me harder. My balls pull up tight, and my cock jerks inside his mouth, unloading deep in his throat as he swallows around me, causing me to come harder.

When I finish, he climbs up, standing between my parted thighs and pulling me in for a kiss, feeding me the taste of my release. "You know how many times I've thought about fucking you on this very desk?"

He groans at that, his hard cock twitching in his shorts as he presses against me. "Why haven't you?"

I reach into his shorts and wrap my hand around his thick length, stroking him and loving the feel of his sticky pre-cum pooling in the slit. He's desperate for it. "We can't here."

He huffs at that, and I kiss his sweet lips again before standing up and spinning us so he's leaning on the desk. After I pull my own pants up, leaving them open, I drop to my knees.

He licks his lips as he looks down at me, and I swear I've never felt more powerful in my life. More seen. More desired. I push his shorts down, watching his cock pop up from the fabric, leaking and flushed red at the tip.

I grip the firm globes of his ass as I lean forward and nuzzle his shaft. One of my fingers slides down his crease. "Would you let me inside you?"

"Oh, fuck yes," he breathes, his hands on my shoulders as he holds himself up.

"I want that so badly."

"Me too," he pants. "Do it." My cock is starting to harden in my pants again, and I know I could. I could bend him over this desk and fuck him until neither of us could move, but I don't.

Instead, I dig my fingers into his ass cheek with one hand and move the other to his dick before I take him into my mouth. I lick and suck, teasing, and then really go for it, sucking hard, making him beg before he lets go and releases hot spurts of cum down my throat.

I lick him clean, moaning at the taste of him, memorizing it with each swallow before I stand up and claim him with another heated kiss. "You can, you know," he says against my lips. "You can have every part of me."

My heart clenches tightly in my chest as I wrap my arms around him. I don't know what to say, but Fletcher—being Fletcher—he doesn't make me say anything. He just kisses me, and then when we separate, he gives me that big beautiful smile.

"Let's go back to your place. I'm starving. You have to feed me."

I grin at that and nod. "Okay. I can do that."

And that's what I keep telling myself. That I can do this, even if I'm already starting to wonder if I truly can.

FLETCHER

I fluff the pillow on the couch for the fiftieth time in the last ten minutes and try to force myself to relax. So Ronan is coming over to my place for the first time. That's totally fine. It's no big deal.

I jump and nearly fall off the damn couch when there's a knock at my door, though, so maybe it is a big deal. I don't know why. Maybe because my mom and siblings break in here often. But I don't think that's it.

I try to catch my breath as I walk to the door and open it, grinning immediately when I see Ronan standing there in slacks and a crisp white button-down shirt. "Don't you ever dress casually?" I tease.

"No," he says instantly, and I'm starting to not mind that curt answer so much, especially since I've also been hearing a lot of *yes's* from him lately.

I want to pull him in for a kiss right away, despite the door still being open and him standing out in the hall, but I think about it and realize that's probably not a great idea in case someone sees.

It's a big deal for him to come over to my place, and I want to make him comfortable. I motion for him to walk inside, and he does before I close and lock the door behind him. Then I'm on him in a hot second, my arms wrapping around his neck as my lips fuse to his.

But no matter how much I want to get him naked, I want other things too. Like to make him dinner. So I slowly pull out of the kiss, nipping and licking at his lips, and okay—it takes me a bit, but I finally extract myself out of his arms and walk around the counter to the stove. "Make yourself at home."

I go to stir the sauce I'd been working on before fluffing the pillows, and he looks around the apartment for a minute, a low whistle sounding from him. "This place is really nice."

He really doesn't sound like he's judging me at all, but I still feel a little bit of shame. "My parents pay for it, remember?"

He offers me a soft smile before taking a seat at the counter and watching me carefully. "I actually think it's really nice that they pay for it after everything you've been through." His smile grows. "It's very economical."

I laugh at that, a real feeling of joy because damn, I really was a shithead to him in his class. I can't believe he didn't kick me out. I turn my back to him to stir the pasta and sauce and murmur, "Rhett never wanted anything. Bree really didn't either. I was the only one who didn't fight Blair on spoiling us."

I stiffen only momentarily when Ronan slides up behind me, his hand on my shoulder, and then I immediately relax into him. "We all process things differently. There's nothing wrong with you wanting to be taken care of, Fletcher."

"I was so tired," I admit. "So damn tired already."

"I know, baby," he says as he wraps his arms around my waist and holds me as I stir the food on the stove. When he nuzzles my neck, I breathe in his expensive, delicious smelling cologne. "This smells incredible," he rasps.

"I was just thinking something like that." I put the spoon down and turn around so I'm facing him, still wrapped up in his strong arms. "It's almost finished."

"You didn't have to cook me dinner."

"I really wanted to," I say as I lean in and kiss his soft lips. Lips I'm addicted to. Lips I dream about when I'm not with him and lips I can't seem to stay away from him when I'm with him.

A timer goes off, startling us both, and then we laugh, quickly moving to grab plates and set up at the counter bar, sitting side by side before we dig in. I've never cooked anyone dinner before, but I actually like to cook. "This is really good," he says as he takes another bite of the pasta.

"I'm glad you like it. Self-taught, you know," I say with a wide grin.

"Your mom didn't teach you?"

I laugh at that. "God, no. Blair does not cook. She can order dinner with the best of them though." I smile, thinking about the few times she's tried to cook over the years, nearly burning the damn house down each time.

"You really love her, don't you?" he asks, a look on his face I can't quite decipher. Is it so odd that I love the woman who adopted me? Maybe. It's not the ending to most of the foster care stories I've ever heard.

"Blair is incredible." I almost say *wait until you meet her*, but I quickly catch myself and bite my tongue. Summer. This is only for summer.

I try to remind myself that, and then before I can move on to another topic, there's a loud knock on my door.

"Oh no," I grumble, and I notice Ronan looks a mix between petrified and amused. I'm sure he's worried about anyone seeing him here, but my instant annoyance is likely amusing to him. "If that's one of my siblings or my mom, I swear."

Yeah, he's definitely smiling now. "Do they knock? I thought they just let themselves in."

Oh shit. He's right. "Well, not always," I say. "Shit."

He stiffens a little bit now. "You don't think it's them?"

"I'm sure it is." I start toward the door. "Maybe they learned manners or something," I try to joke, but then there's another bang on the door.

"Hey, Fletcher, you home?" My eyes widen at the sound of Josh's voice. *Josh. What the hell?*

"I, umm . . ." Ronan is still seated, but his arms are crossed as he watches me.

He's probably waiting for an explanation, but I don't have one. *What is he doing here?* I sigh. "Yeah, I'm here. Just a second," I holler through the door and look over at Ronan. "So . . . it's Josh."

Ronan is watching me carefully. Obviously, he doesn't know who Josh is.

"He's a friend." Sure, that's a good way to describe him. "He's safe. I promise, okay? He doesn't go to this school or anything, so we have nothing to worry about," I try to assure him because his safety is everything to me. "But I can send him away. Don't worry," I babble like an idiot.

"Fletcher." I look over at Ronan, who's pretty damn calm while I'm here freaking the hell out. I have no idea why the hell he would be here. I haven't talked to him in months. "Breathe and open the door for your *friend.*" Something about the way he said *friend* makes it clear he knows something is up.

But honestly, that's the only way I can really describe Josh. We fooled around a couple of times, but we were never lovers. We didn't date. Hell, we barely talked. We probably can't even be called actual friends. *Acquaintances who bang? Is that a thing?*

"Fletcher." I look back over at Ronan and realize my thoughts have gone rogue. He nods toward the door. "The door."

"Right." I make my way over to the door and pull it open just a crack. Ronan didn't seem too worried about being seen, but I still feel myself wanting to protect him.

Josh is standing there, staring at me with wide exasperated eyes. He tosses his hands up. "Finally! I didn't think you were going to answer, man."

"Uh, sorry," I say awkwardly because it definitely crossed my mind to not answer it, thinking maybe he'd just go away. "What's up?"

"I was in town and super fucking horny. Thought I'd stop by, and we could bang one out." I make some sort of choked noise, and I swear—though it has to be my imagination—but I swear I hear a low growl coming from inside my apartment.

"I, uh . . ." I stand there, frozen in this awkward sort of limbo. This is so not happening.

95

But then I hear footsteps coming up behind me before the door is opened wider. Ronan stands by my side. "Aren't you going to introduce me to your *friend?*" Again, the word *friend* has an emphasis, telling me he thinks we're more.

And Josh's loud mouth all but just confirmed that. Josh's eyes widen as he stares at Ronan. "Woah, dude. I didn't realize you had company. Sorry about that."

"It's fine," I say it, but I don't mean it. I like Josh. He's a decent guy, but I also want him to go the hell away so I can go back to eating dinner with my professor. "Josh, this is ummmm . . ." I turn to Ronan, not really sure how to introduce him.

"Ronan," Ronan supplies, reaching his hand out for Josh.

Josh grins and shakes his hand. "Nice to meet you. I'm Josh." Josh turns to look at me. "Didn't know you were dating anyone."

I'm about to tell him we aren't dating before Ronan freaks the hell out, but Ronan surprises me and speaks up first. "It's new."

Josh nods his head, but I can't help gawking at Ronan. Did he just say we're dating? I mean, I know he did it for Josh's benefit, although, I'm not totally sure why, but still. My mind does a little happy jig, despite myself.

Only for the summer. Only for the summer. Only for the summer.

I chant that phrase over and over again and nearly miss Ronan inviting Josh inside my place for dinner. "Oh, I couldn't impose."

I'm about to accept that and usher Josh out of the apartment, but Ronan won't have it. "It's not a big deal. Come in. It's good to get to know Fletcher's friends."

He's got to be kidding.

Josh doesn't seem to care, though, because he just barrels into the apartment and helps himself to a big portion of the pasta, plopping his ass down next to Ronan. I close the door and walk slowly over to my seat.

"So how do you two know each other?" Ronan asks Josh casually, and I just want to scream. Surely, if Josh doesn't talk, he can stuff his face sooner and I can get him out of here.

I should feel guilty about that, but damn it, all I have is the summer with Ronan. I want every single second.

"Oh, we went to high school together," Josh says with a mouth full of food. "And his brother is attached at the hip to my best friend."

"Ah, I see," Ronan says politely.

"And you know, we used to bang. But I'm guessing that's over."

I chose the wrong moment to take a bite and nearly choke on my food. And I swear I hear that low, deadly growl again. "It is."

I look at Ronan, surprised by him staking his claim, but Josh seems totally unaffected, still stuffing his mouth with food.

"I need to use the restroom," Ronan announces and stands up from his seat. He turns to me. "Show me?"

"Oh, right." I stand up too before looking at Josh. "I'll be right back."

He waves me off, grabbing a breadstick, and I chuckle. Goofy bastard. I actually do consider him a friend, I realize as I lead Ronan back to my room where my bathroom is. I could have shown him to the small bathroom off the kitchen, but I wanted to explain myself a little first.

But when we get to my room, I don't get a word in before my body is slammed against the wall, and his large, warm body is blanketing my, his firm lips fusing to mine as he devours my mouth.

Okay. We don't need to talk.

I wrap my arms around him and kiss him back, my mouth accepting his plundering tongue as his hands go into my hair and lay claim, his fingers gripping my strands. "Okay, I thought you were mad at me," I breathe heavily against his lips, kissing him again after getting those few words out.

His kiss grows softer, and soon he stops it all together, resting his forehead against mine. "Friends?"

"We had a couple of hookups, but it was nothing. I haven't been with him since Christmas, and I have no idea what he's doing here."

"Okay," he says so simply I want to scream.

"Okay?"

He sighs and then pushes away from me, stepping back. "I'm not used to this, Fletcher."

"Used to what?" I ask, genuinely confused.

He huffs, throwing his hands up in frustration before pushing one of them through his hair. "Being jealous. Or possessive. That's not . . ." He drops his hand and shakes his head. "I don't get that way, but as soon as I heard him say that he was here to fuck you, I couldn't control myself. Growling like a fucking dog."

So that wasn't my imagination. I walk closer to him. "It was hot." I shrug it off with a grin.

He pins me with an annoyed look. "No. It wasn't. I'm an adult. I know how to use words."

"So why did you invite him in?" I have to ask because he has to know I'd have been on board sending poor Josh on his way.

"I was trying to be an adult," he says as he starts to pace, and God help me, he's really cute like this. All discombobulated and truly annoyed with himself, it seems. "But then he started talking about fucking you, and again, I wanted to mark my damn territory."

"Well, thanks for not pissing on my leg," I try to joke.

He looks distressed though. "Fletcher . . ." His eyes meet mine, and I move to him, my hands going to his hips.

"It's okay. I wouldn't like anyone talking about being with you either."

"But—" he starts to say, but I can't hear it again right now. I can't hear that it ends with summer. I press my lips to his in a soft, devastating kiss.

"But nothing." I pull back enough to look into his eyes. "Let's go finish dinner and kick Josh out." I grin, and he laughs.

"You're a terrible friend."

I shrug. "I'm okay with it," I say honestly.

He presses another kiss to my mouth before he takes my hand, and we go back out to the main room. Josh has cleaned his plate, and he looks amused when we walk out with our hair messy, our clothes rumpled, and our lips still glistening with each other's saliva, but he doesn't really call us on it.

"Well, thanks for dinner. I should get out of your hair," he says just as we both sit down to eat.

"You don't have to rush off," Ronan says, but I don't hear any hint of him actually meaning that, and I don't think Josh does either.

"Yeah, I better get going." He stands up, and I do too so I can walk him to the door.

"Sorry about this," I say as I open the door, even though I'm not really sure what I'm sorry for. He did show up unannounced, and I fed him. But he was hoping for some no-strings-attached sex, and he didn't get that so yeah. Sorry works.

"You seem happy, man," he says with a bright grin.

It takes everything in me not to glance back at Ronan. "I'm always happy."

Josh chuckles and shakes his head. "Sure, man. Well, see you around, I suppose."

I nod, and he leaves with a quick wave in Ronan's direction. I close and lock the door before heading back over to finish dinner with my man.

No.

Not my man.

But *my summer man* doesn't sound good.

"So that happened," I say awkwardly, and Ronan laughs.

"Is this what it's always like at your place?"

I want to say no, but I don't lie to him. "Yup. I'm sure my mom or one of my siblings will be busting through the door any damn minute."

Ronan laughs at that, but then tosses his napkin onto the counter and stands up, taking my hand. "Then we should probably get to the good stuff now."

I smile just as his lips meet mine for a kiss. "Sounds like a plan."

As we make our way to my room again, I can't stop thinking about the future. How it would be if we lasted after summer. Having meals at my place, my mom or Josh or someone else busting in but it not really mattering because we have more than just a few months.

Is it really so damn bad to want that?

99

Ronan starts to undress me slowly, his lips back on mine in an instant, but then he's pulling back and looking into my eyes before his gaze drifts over my body, then back up to my face. The way he watches me . . . it's like he has so many things he wants to say to me.

So many things he won't let himself say. He's put up a wall. He knows everything about me, but he still doesn't allow himself to tell me much about him. All I know is how important his job is to him.

A stinging sensation in my gut feels an awful lot like guilt because what I'd be asking for if we went past these few months could jeopardize that. Could take away his career that he clings to so fiercely. That he loves.

Summer.

I can't let myself think there will ever be anything else.

This is all we have.

RONAN

I'm totally out of my element here. I don't know what's happening to me. I've had hookups in the past. Short flings. No big deal. They served a purpose until they ran their course.

But for whatever reason, meeting Fletcher's friend Josh last night has left me spinning. I've never felt jealousy in my life, but there's no denying that's exactly what I felt when stupid Josh opened his stupid mouth and talked about fucking my Fletcher.

My Fletcher.

Jesus fucking Christ.

I'm going to start beating my chest and chanting "mine" soon.

This is absolutely ridiculous. And I couldn't keep my hands off him last night. We wound up in a mess of sweat and cum, collapsed on his bed before I convinced him to come and shower with me. Making another mess as we ground our cocks together until we were both crying out with yet another release.

We wound back up in his bed, but when I woke up to disturbing thoughts of him and stupid Josh in the middle of the night, I wound up waking him up too. My mouth on him brought him to his third orgasm of the night before we passed the hell out.

I had some work to do today, so I reluctantly pried myself away from him this morning. But he's coming over to my place this evening, and my heart is racing with the anticipation of seeing him as I prepare dinner for us.

I don't know what the hell is happening to me.

But it doesn't stop me from practically racing to the door as soon as I hear the doorbell ring and flinging it open. Fletcher's warm smile greets me, and I yank him inside, barely managing to get the door closed before my mouth is on his.

He kisses me back, but only for a moment before he pulls back, a mischievous grin on his handsome face. "Missed me, huh?"

I'm sure he's expecting me to argue, but I can't seem to. "I think I did."

He looks surprised, blinking in shock, before he laughs. "I knew I'd grow on you."

"Mm-hmm," I murmur halfheartedly, even though it's kind of true. How the hell it happened, I'm not sure, but I'd be lying if I said I've thought about anything else today. My thoughts were consumed with Fletcher. "Help me in the kitchen?"

His smile is so damn bright, it's nearly blinding, but he follows me into the kitchen, not saying another word. We fall seamlessly into making a salad together, cutting up fresh vegetables and putting them in the bowl.

"You know . . ." He chops up a tomato, adding most of it to the salad, but popping a piece into his mouth and chewing it as his eyes meet mine. "I missed you too."

I want to mock him for that, but damn it, it does something really funny to my insides. I don't know what the hell he's doing to me, and before I can say anything, I hear a notification on his phone.

He reaches into his pocket and grins. A moment of unwelcome, nearly shocking jealousy spreads through me. *Please don't be stupid Josh who's making him smile like that.*

I don't look.

And I don't ask.

I stand there like an idiot as he types something on his phone and then places it on the counter. When he looks over at me, I don't look away fast enough, and he knows I was watching him.

"My sister, Bree," he supplies, and a whoosh of relief goes through me. Wow. This is really getting out of hand.

"She's shopping with my mom but sent me a picture of my dad carrying their shopping bags." The fond smile on his face is a glimpse into the real Fletcher. The one he hid with his arrogant bravado for so long.

"You all are really close."

He goes back to chopping tomatoes. "We are."

"You going to be okay when she goes to New York?" I don't know why I'm asking. Honestly, we should have skipped dinner and just gone right to the bedroom. Keep it simple and easy. Just sex for this summer loophole.

But I want to know more about him. I crave it. Which is a total mindfuck.

I watch him, though, and his face morphs into that cocky fuckboy smile I really don't miss. "Of course I will."

"Don't do that." And again, why the hell am I going on? I should just drop it. Summer flings don't care about you hiding your feelings.

"Do what?" he asks, and his fake smile almost slips.

"You don't have to hide your feelings from me." *Shit. Shit. Shit.*

Yes, he does. He should. He should run, damn it. I should run. Feelings. Yuck.

He looks like he's going to argue with me, and part of me is cheering him on to do just that. *Tell me feelings are gross, Fletcher. Say you don't have them. That this is just sex and I need to chill.*

Sadly, though, he doesn't say any of those things to drag me back to reality. "I'm not hiding. I'll be fine." I just stare at him, waiting for the rest of it because there's more to it, and we both know it. Apparently, I care. Damn him. So I wait. And then he huffs, "Fine. I'm so damn happy for her. So happy. But we've never been that far apart since we met. I used to panic when she got placed somewhere over two miles from me, and now, she's going to fucking New York. I'm freaking out a lot about it."

I offer him a gentle smile. "Was that so hard?"

He tosses a crouton at me, and I catch it with my hand and pop it into my mouth. "Yes, it was," he answers with another haughty little huff.

"It really will be okay, you know?"

He sighs and then nods. "Yeah. She's so damn excited. I can't help but feel happy for her. She's tough too."

The oven timer goes off, and I start to remove the chicken, but I'm still focused on Fletcher. "Tell me about her?"

He looks momentarily surprised but then recovers quickly. "Bree's the strongest woman I know, besides my mom. She doesn't take shit from anyone, but she's the first to offer help to anyone who needs it. I think Rhett and I always thought we needed to take care of her, but looking back, it was always Bree who took care of us."

I place the pan on the stovetop and turn off the oven, turning to look over at Fletcher, who's so damn beautiful doing nothing but standing in my kitchen, wearing his ridiculous tank top and shorts. "Sounds like you all took care of each other. It couldn't have been easy in foster care," I say grimly, my own demons threatening to come back up.

And I think he notices because his eyes turn almost stormy as he approaches me. "When are you going to tell me something about *you*?"

Well shit. This whole wanting to know more about him thing really backfired, didn't it?

"You know plenty of somethings about me," I try, turning away and grabbing two plates from the cupboard.

"Really?"

My shoulders drop, and I turn around to look at him. "What do you want from me, Fletcher?" I ask quietly because I know deep down what he wants.

"You know everything about me. I mean, everything. Things I really don't talk about. Things I don't tell anyone. I've let you see the real me, but you haven't shown me anything." He drops his hands to my hips, looking right into my eyes and not backing down, but there's a gentleness in his gaze. "Just give me something. Anything at all. I know it's just for the summer or whatever," he says softly, and I can hear the sad disappointment in his words, which slashes my heart right open. "But just something."

"Fine." I try to think of something I can tell him. Something no one else knows. My gut turns, and darkness starts to take over, my knees starting to go weak. But I push it away. Nope. I'm not going there.

Fletcher drops his hands from my hips and gives me a sad little nod. "Okay. Dinner."

That plastic fake smile is back on his face, and I hate it so damn much, I blurt out, "I'm terrified of potatoes."

He was facing away from me, probably getting the salad to take to the table, but he stops and then slowly turns around. "What?"

"I know it sounds dumb, but it's a legit fear. Not really potatoes, but those white gross . . ." I almost gag, just thinking about them. I wave my hand, trying to push the visual out of my head. "I can't do it. I hate when they start growing that shit on them."

He's watching me closely, one eyebrow raised. "Are you messing with me?"

"No. I swear," I say honestly. "I've never told another soul about it because I know I'll get teased relentlessly, but I swear it's true. I don't even keep potatoes in the house. If I want potatoes for dinner, I have to buy them that day, in person, after examining them, and if I don't use them, I toss them."

A slow smile takes over his face, and then he lets out a quick, small laugh. "Sorry." He schools his reaction and walks closer to me. "Thank you for trusting me with your secret."

I cup his face in my hands and look into his blue orbs. "I want to tell you more. I do," I say, pain creeping up in my chest, just thinking about anything deeper than my very real fear of rotting potatoes.

He leans forward, my hands still on his face, and presses a kiss to my lips. "Thank you."

I smile against his lips, and he kisses me again before we part to have dinner in my dining room.

He seems content, but I still hate that I couldn't let him in.

But I also hate that I really, really wanted to.

It's just for the summer.

FLETCHER

He's afraid of potatoes.

I can't help the goofy-ass grin on my face as I help Annie do some research in the library. I mean, I asked him to give me something, and he did.

Yup. My face might actually split open with how big I'm grinning right now. To some, it may have seemed like a joke or not enough, but to me? He's trying. Why? I'm not sure either of us will actually admit it.

Me for fear of being wrong and him for just . . . well, fear.

But he was dead serious. I could tell by the look on his face as he desperately searched for something to tell me. Something very real about himself. Something he doesn't tell other people.

It may seem small, but I know there's so much more to him than he lets on. I have no idea what he's hiding about his past, but there's something there. I recognize that pain.

So yeah, I'm a smiling goofy bastard today after Professor Ronan Barlowe shared his secret with me last night.

Annie closes her laptop and peers at me over the table. "Go see him."

"What?" I say, looking at her over my still open laptop. "Who?" She can't know what I was thinking about. There's no way. I mean, we haven't been super careful, but we've been pretty damn careful. Unless maybe she saw me coming out of his office a couple of times.

She rolls her eyes at me with a sweet laugh. "Do you really think I'm that dense?"

Oh shit. She does know. I'm pretty sure my jaw has hit the floor as I stare at her like a dead fish, my mouth just hanging open.

She reaches across the table and closes my laptop, her eyes lighting up with amusement and maybe a little bit of pity. "Go see him. We're done today, and I won't need your help until Tuesday. Go."

My throat is dry, and nerves are threatening to eat me alive, but this is normally where I thrive. I'm usually good at hiding a part of myself, but I can't seem to do that at all with Ronan, and apparently that seems to trickle down to his friends too. Because I know how important his friends are to him, I can't try to lie to her. "Does he know you know?"

She laughs at that and then she shakes her head. "No. Of course not. He'd freak the hell out and probably try to end things with you." She waves her hand. "He gets really damn dramatic sometimes."

I can't help the smile, even though the thought of him ending anything makes me sick to my stomach. *He's going to end things when the summer ends,* my mind tries to remind me. I push it away. "You aren't upset?"

"About you and him?" I nod. "No, of course not. Look, I love Ronan, but he thinks too much. He overthinks way too much, and you're good for him."

"Because I don't think about anything?" I ask with a grin.

Her eyes roll. "No. But you make him more fun. I haven't been around him much lately—I'm guessing that's because of you—" I should feel guilty, but I don't. And she only laughs and then goes on, "But when I have seen him, he's been so happy. Lighter. It's so good to see him that way and so rare."

My chest pinches with the information. "He is kind of wound tight."

Her lips are pursed tightly now, and it's like she wants to tell me something but stops herself. Has he told her about his past? I won't betray his trust by asking, not that she'd tell me anything, but it only makes me want to know even more. "You make him happy. You should go. You know, he's in his office, and if you don't make him leave, he'll probably stay there all damn night."

I smile at that because she's right. "It's just for the summer, you know?" I blurt out as I stand up.

She cocks her head to the side and studies me. I wait for her response. Why I need it I'm not sure, and I'm not sure what I'm hoping she'll say. *Maybe she'll think it's possible to last longer. That there's some hope.*

She just sits up a little straighter, lifting her chin and looking into my eyes. "Then make it the best summer."

Well, damn. Okay, so no hope from Annie, but she's right. If it's only going to be the summer, I'm going to make sure it's going to be the best damn summer.

I thank her, and on my short walk over to Ronan's office, a plan is already forming. My stomach is in knots by the time I reach his office door and knock on the frame to let him know I'm there.

He looks up from his computer, sitting at his desk, and the smile that comes over his face nearly knocks me over. It's so damn beautiful, it hurts.

Please don't say no.

"Done for the day?" he asks as I walk into the room. I don't shut the door behind me—I kind of think at this point that may look more suspicious than anything, and if he says yes, hopefully we won't be staying here long anyway.

"I am." I stop at his desk, my heart about to leap out of my chest.

"I'm almost finished. I was thinking about watching that Netflix doc about the couple who was kidnapped."

Again with the goofy-ass grin. I just can't seem to help myself. I'm way too far gone. I know I am, but still, Annie's right. I need to make the most out of this summer. The memories of this . . . that's what's going to make the heartache worth it.

"Come away with me," I blurt out, and he is, of course, a little taken aback because who the hell wouldn't be when someone blurts a command like that out of nowhere? *Jesus, Fletcher.*

"Where?" He's super careful when he asks me this.

"My brother's boyfriend, Grayson, has this pretty nice house by the lake. He said we could use it for the weekend." Well okay, he'll say it's fine, I'm sure. He's made us all a key and said we can use it when we want to. I'll send him a text later to make sure it's cool, but I know for a fact they're going to be at their place in the city this weekend and not at the lake. So it's fine.

He cocks an eyebrow at me, still watching me carefully. "Where is this coming from?"

Fear. Wanting. The nearly crippling need to have as much time with him as possible before the summer ends.

I don't answer him that way though—you know, with the truth. "I thought it would be nice to get away." And it would be. God, I want this more and more as I stare at him, knowing I can't touch him right now the way I want to. That someone could see. We always have to be on alert.

I want a weekend where that's not the case.

"Think about it. You have one class tomorrow, and it's at the butt-crack of dawn. The house is a four-hour drive. We could be there around one in the afternoon. You don't have a Monday class. We can get back that evening." He doesn't seem to be against it yet, so I keep talking. "It would be kind of nice to go somewhere no one knows us. We could just do whatever we want. Hell, we could hold hands out in public."

A small smile falls over his lips, and I blush a little. "You want to hold my hand?"

"Shut up," I say with absolutely no bite in it. "The way Rhett and Grayson talk about this place . . ." I bite my bottom lip and worry I'm giving away too much of myself but barrel on because that's what I do. "It was good for them at their beginning." Ronan's eyes widen, and I know why. I hold a hand up. "Not that this is a beginning of some-thing, I just mean . . ." *Shit, Fletcher. Shut. Up.*

He stands and walks closer to me, his face deadly serious, and I'm almost certain I've botched the hell out of this. That he's going to just end it now because I'm clearly a super clingy mess, but instead he brushes a hand over my cheek and smiles. "It sounds amazing."

"Really?" I barely squeak.

"Yeah. I think . . ." He sighs, his hands twitching a little at his sides, and I wonder if it's because he wants to touch me again. God, I hope that's the reason. Because I'm fully gone for this man.

It would help me feel like less of an idiot if he had even a little of that going on.

"I think it would be really great, Fletcher. Are you sure it's okay with your brother and his boyfriend?"

"Yes," I say instantly. "Let's go pack so we can leave right from here tomorrow," I say far too excitedly, but he's saying yes. I'm too excited to contain myself.

He chuckles. "Okay. Let's go."

I can't believe he said yes, but I'm not going to waste any damn time worrying about that.

He said yes, and we're going to the lake house tomorrow.

For whatever reason, this feels huge. And I'm here for it.

RONAN

This feels like a really bad decision, but when Fletcher came into my office yesterday, all hopped-up on obvious nerves, and asked me to go with him, I couldn't say no. Though I know I should.

But I can't remember the last time I did something for me. Just for my own pleasure. Not because I had to do it to survive, but simply because I wanted to, and damn it, I wanted to.

So badly.

So I said yes, and now I'm in the passenger seat of his Jeep while he munches on beef jerky as he drives, occasionally singing along with the radio, and it may be the cutest damn thing I've ever seen.

What the hell is happening to me?

When we reach the Ozarks, it is in fact around one in the afternoon, and Fletcher parks his Jeep in front of a really nice, fairly good-sized house by the lake and turns the vehicle off. "We're here."

I look up at the house. "It's nice."

He grins. "Not impressed yet?"

"I didn't say that." I turn to look at him, wanting to say so many things. Like I wouldn't care if it was a dilapidated shack he brought me to as long as he was here with me, but I don't let that come out of my mouth.

Summer.

This is for the summer only. I can't get blinded by this . . . God, what do you even call it? Chemistry? We definitely have off-the-charts chemistry. But it feels like even more than that.

I try to shake that off. Push it away because it can't happen, and he must sense I'm struggling with something because he pushes open his door. "Come on, Professor. I'll show you around."

I don't even hate when he says *Professor* like that anymore. Except for it most certainly does things to my dick. And after last night and this morning in the shower, you'd think I'd be sated.

But I'm starting to truly worry I'll never get enough of him.

Oh, how things have changed.

We grab our bags, and he lets us into the house. It's nice, but it's not overly fancy. It's cozy. I can definitely see the charm to it.

"So I'm pretty sure Rhett and Grayson use the loft room up there." He points upward, and I see a spiral staircase leading up to a room, then look back at Fletcher. "And I'm not touching that. So we should stay in one of the other rooms."

I grin. "Sounds good."

He leads me down the hall to a fairly large bedroom with an attached bathroom. "Blair may have convinced Grayson to let her add on a couple of rooms recently. He can't say no to her either."

His mom sounds like she's really something else. And I can't help thinking that I really want to meet her someday. My heart clenches tightly in my chest so hard I actually rub my hand over that spot.

I don't even bother reminding myself that we only have the summer. Fletcher places his bag on the bed, and I do the same before he turns to me, his smile bright and infectious.

It takes my mind off the gloom and doom it was on, and then his lips meet mine, and it takes all of two seconds to completely forget what I was upset about.

"I can't believe you agreed to come here with me," he says against my lips, and it breaks my heart. I've been such an asshole to him. And not just before I really started to get to know him, but even recently.

Because he's let me in. Despite everything that's happened in his life. Despite being abandoned by people who should have cared about him the most. He's good. He's so infinitely good, and he still has trust.

He trusts me.

And I haven't given him anything back.

It's not fair at all, and I want to tell him everything about me. I want to fully explain why I'm such a closed-off asshole, but I can't get the words out. And not only because Fletcher currently has his tongue shoved in my mouth, his flesh sweeping over mine. His hard body is pressed up against me as his fingers glide through my hair.

I want to tell him.

But of course, I don't. I let myself get lost in his kiss and his touch. I take my time pulling his tank top up and over his head before I kiss every inch of his bare torso. His muscles flex as I drag my tongue through the lines of his sculpted abs. He tips his head back as I lower to my knees in front of him, his hands on my shoulders as I remove his shoes and lower his shorts.

His cock springs free because he wasn't wearing any underwear. He kicks the shorts away as I stare at his steely length, the tip glistening with arousal. "Goddamn, that's hot," I breathe as I grasp his hard shaft in my hand, slowly stroking him.

"Oh fuck. Please, Ronan." I smile.

"Oh, you're begging me, huh?" I have to tease him a little bit. I run my tongue down the length of his erection, swirling it around the tip, but not staying there too long before I drag my tongue down the other side of him.

"Please," he gasps again.

I'll never tire of the raspy sound of ecstasy coming from Fletcher. I don't put him out of his misery just yet though. Instead, I kiss both of his hip bones, one and then the other, my hand on his shaft but not moving. My tongue trails over his thigh and down to his heavy balls, swirling around them and teasing before I take one and then the other into my mouth.

"Ronan," he gasps. "I want to come." His fingers dig into my shoulder. "I need to come."

He's desperate for it, panting heavily, his hips thrusting forward, trying to get some relief from my hand. When I finally take pity on him and take him into my mouth, he lets out a relieved curse, one of his hands going into my hair. "Yes. Just like that. Please, Ronan. Please please please," he chants as he punches his hips forward.

I let him fuck my throat until it's aching, but I don't care because watching Fletcher take his pleasure is the sexiest thing I've ever experienced.

"I'm so close. So damn close." He sounds breathless, and I can't resist reaching into my shorts—yes, I'm actually wearing shorts today, and I'm not even planning on running. Of course, he teased me a little when he saw I was wearing a t-shirt and shorts instead of a suit and tie, but I think he liked it. And I'm for sure grateful I did now. The ease of my hand going under the waistband of my shorts is a relief when I wrap my hand around my aching cock.

I stroke as he fucks my mouth with his long cock, and when I swallow around him, that's when he lets go, crying my name as warm cum fills my mouth. The taste of him is what sets off my own orgasm, making a mess in my shorts, but I couldn't care less.

He pulls me up to him, slamming his mouth to mine as we kiss and then fall to the bed, not missing a beat. Despite being sticky with cum and our cocks being soft, we kiss and kiss some more. His hands slide through my hair, and I feel every single thing deep inside my chest as his lips remain on mine.

We say so many things in this kiss. Things I so desperately want to say out loud but haven't allowed myself to do it. He's fully naked, and I'm still clothed with a mess in my shorts, but I can't stop kissing him.

I don't want to. The things he makes me feel are unlike anything I've ever experienced. I spent so much of my life being closed-off and not trusting anyone. Then he just barreled his way into my life and opened me in ways I've never experienced.

"Shower with me," he breathes against my lips, and I barely manage a nod before he pulls me away from the bed, but my lips are still seeking his out as we make our way to the bathroom. He manages to get the shower on and my clothes off, and the whole time, I cling to him.

Terrified to let him go for even a second. I'm desperate and needy. So unlike me. But I don't take the time to worry about it. We wash each other as we kiss, and when he turns off the shower, I grab a soft fluffy towel on the rack and dry him off and then myself, and then it's back to the bed.

His kiss is soft and exploring, but it seems like he's not ready to let me go just yet either, and I'm more than fine with that.

"My mother was really young when she had me," I blurt out, and Fletcher slowly backs away from my mouth, pulling back a little but enough to look into my eyes with surprise.

"What?"

I realize this is super awkward timing while we're lying naked in bed and kissing, but for some reason, I have to tell him this. I need him to know me—really know me. "She was really young. Way too damn young to have me."

He takes a deep breath, and it's like he understands what's happening now, a look of peace coming over his features as he tucks his hands under his cheek and stares at me as we lie on our sides.

"Her parents were super religious, I guess, and kicked her out when they found out she was pregnant."

"I'm sure that's what Jesus would do," Fletcher quips and then gives me a sheepish smile. "Sorry."

"Yeah, my thoughts exactly. But she tried. I think," I add because I've just been told these things. I obviously don't have the memories of that time. "We crashed on her friend's couch. Different friends. When one would get sick of her having a baby around all the time, we'd move to another one. She quit school and was trying to work, but it was always hard to find someone to watch me."

His brow furrows, but he doesn't say anything. He seems perfectly content to just listen as I talk.

"When I was four, apparently, she lost me at the mall. She wanted to hang out with her friends, and I was probably being a brat, so she thought it would be fine to just leave me in an arcade for an hour or two while she walked around with her friends."

He looks horrified, and I was too when I read it in my file. Because

I don't have a memory of that either. Though sometimes, I think when I dream about it, it's actually a memory.

"The cops and CPS were called, but she just had to take some classes, and she did. She kept custody of me. But then a year later, she left me at this shitty place where we were staying while she went out on a date." Fletcher's face looks pained, but I keep going, "I kind of remember this, although it's foggy. I remember being in pain and crying. I had cut my foot on a piece of glass, and it was bleeding really bad."

"Jesus," he breathes.

"My mom's friend, who we were staying with, came home and saw the blood. Thankfully, she took me to the hospital. They tried to reach my mom, but it took her a while to show up. When she got there, the cops talked to her. She made excuses, I guess. I didn't really get to hear it. I just wanted to leave the hospital and go with my mom. But there were a lot of adults telling me that might not happen for a while."

"They put you into foster care," he says, his voice full of despair.

"She left," I say, but I barely get the words out because the pain I felt that day has creeped back up. It nearly chokes me. This is why I don't talk about it. Why I hate thinking about it. That darkness was nearly impossible to claw my way out of then. I'm always afraid when it comes up, I won't be able to make my way out of it again.

"What do you mean?"

"She just left me there. I don't know if she asked for a break from talking to the cops, but she just ran. She never came back. They tried to track her down, but yes . . ." I meet his eyes. "They put me into foster care."

He looks like he's having trouble breathing now, and his eyes are watery. "You were a foster kid."

"They tried to get my grandparents to take me, but they wanted nothing to do with me." I try like hell to swallow—my throat is sore with all the emotions I feel. They didn't want me. "I was a ward of the state at that time."

"I'm so damn sorry, Ronan," he says, and when he does, I know he really understands. He was the same. He knows what it's like to not be wanted by the people who should want you the most. To feel so damn lost and scared.

I think that's why, when I finally stopped and listened to him, when I heard his real truth, the sparks flew. Why I couldn't keep myself from kissing him that day because it's so damn rare to have that sort of connection.

"Why didn't you tell me?" There's no anger in his tone. He just really wants to know why.

"When I talk about it, it makes it real. I've spent a lot of time trying to forget, Fletcher. I push people away, so I don't have to talk about it. Every single day, I wake up and think I'm back in that hell. That I never got out."

He makes some sort of choked sound, and then he's pushing into my arms. I wrap my arms around him and hold him to me. "No one rescued you." It's not a question. It's a statement, and I realize why he says it.

"I'm okay. I made it out."

He pulls back a little, but stays in my arms, just looking up at me. "How?"

I fought.

FLETCHER

He was a foster kid. Never in a million years would I have seen that coming, but now everything is starting to make so much sense. Why he was so angry when he thought I was just a spoiled rich kid.

Why he hardly ever smiled and kept people at bay. His reaction when he heard I was a foster kid.

No one rescued him.

"As soon as I could, I got a job. It was usually just side jobs, getting paid under the table, but I hustled. Every single day of my life, I fucking hustled."

I swallow hard because I know. I know what it was like. We told ourselves we'd find a way out. I remember sitting for hours with Bree and Rhett, talking about all the ways we could make money and save up. Make a life for ourselves. Get the hell out of foster care. That was our one goal.

"And I kept my grades exceptionally high, which thankfully wasn't that hard for me. I worked, and I saved. And when I was sixteen, I finally had enough saved to get a crappy apartment and get myself emancipated."

"They granted it?"

He nods. "They did. I'd started working at this little diner by the school. I had six months of employment there and a stellar attendance record both at work and school. My grades were high. I didn't give that judge one reason to deny me."

I smile sadly at that because I can picture sixteen-year-old Ronan —no-nonsense and just presenting the facts to the judge. Daring them to question his ability to take care of himself.

"You rescued yourself," I say, guilt washing over me. Guilt I've felt since the day I realized I was going to be adopted by Blair and Rhys. That I didn't have to be scared any longer. But there were so many other kids out there who didn't get that. Who had to spend every single day scared and alone. Hungry.

"Hey." His deep voice makes me realize I'd looked away from him, and I look back up and into his eyes. "Don't do that."

"Do what?" I ask a tad defensively.

"Just because someone adopted you doesn't make your suffering any less valid. You went through hell too."

Damn him. "But I got out."

"So did I." He says it so firmly, I want to believe him, but I can see the scars now. The ones on his soul. From the time he spent in hell. "Fletcher, I'm okay. I made it."

"But you had to work your ass off to do it." My voice sounds strangled and tired. "No wonder you hated me." I shake my head. God, I think about the days I sauntered into his class, acting like I didn't have a care in the world. Acting like I owned the place.

"I didn't hate you. Not even a little bit, Fletcher. Maybe I was a little jealous of what I thought was freedom to not have to worry, but now I know you. I know what you were doing."

"And what was that?" I ask, knowing he's already figured me out. Knowing without a doubt he sees right through my charade.

"Surviving," he surprises me, and my eyes widen.

"I was a shithead."

He offers a really small smile, one that doesn't reach his eyes, but he shakes his head. "So was I. I pushed people away, so I didn't have to talk about my past, and you did something totally different." He sounds almost in awe. "You found a way to pull people in, charming them into thinking you're okay."

"It was fake," I say. "I'm a fucking fraud."

"No," he says and then uses his hand to tip my chin up. I guess I looked away from him again. "You're the most real human I've ever met."

He leans and presses a firm kiss against my lips. "Tell me more," I plead because I want to know everything now that he's opened up. I know it's greedy, but I can't bring myself to care. I need this.

"I loved that shitty little apartment I had, but I lived in constant fear that something would happen and I'd get kicked out. I went ahead and took my GED so I could apply to colleges and passed on the first try. I went to college and worked my ass off every single day." He gives a small laugh. "I don't think I slept for years. I worked several jobs while going to school because I had some grants but not nearly enough to pay for school, and I didn't want to start my life off in a ton of debt. In graduate school, I was able to get a teaching assistantship, which paid for my school and gave me just enough to squeak by, but it was a lot of work."

"You're incredible." And I mean that. I'm in absolute awe of him.

He just shrugs. "I knew from a young age I couldn't depend on anyone else. So I just kept going, and when I finally graduated, I got a job almost immediately at the college. I bought my house two years later, and it needed a lot of work, but I didn't care. It was mine."

I smile sadly at that, tears pooling in my eyes because it's all clicking into place now. "It was yours."

He nods, and I see the hint of pride in his smile. "I worked some side jobs while teaching for a few years because I just wanted to feel safe. For the first time in my life, I felt really, truly safe. Like no one could take it away from me."

"That's why you're so afraid to lose your job," I say, knowing that's it. And God, do I get it. As foster kids, we move around so much. All we want is security.

While other kids dream about a gaming system or new technology, we're dreaming about a roof over our heads and a full belly where no one will hurt us or call us names. Where we're safe and taken care of.

"You mean a lot to me, Fletcher." His voice sounds so damn pained, and I reach up, my hand resting on his face.

"I get it. I really do. That house is yours. You made your escape, and it's your sanctuary."

"And the job pays for that house. And for me to never have to rely on another human again."

My heart sinks because I know why it has to end with the summer. Why we absolutely cannot risk his job. This is everything to him, more so than most people. It's a very tightly strung rope, keeping him from breaking.

"Thank you for telling me," I say, moving my body up so I'm face-to-face with him, and then before he says anything else, I steal into his mouth. It's all too damn raw. I think I've found my soulmate, believe it or not, I really truly do, and I have to let him go.

But not quite yet.

I have him for now, and I'm not going to waste it. I kiss him, and it doesn't take long before the seriousness of the talk fades and our bodies start to respond. My dick is aching, my balls full and begging for release by the time he pushes me onto my back and climbs onto me.

"Ronan," I say against his lips. "Please."

I can feel him smiling against my mouth. "Please what?"

"I need you inside me," I say it in a quiet, pleading rasp, and it's enough to make him pull back and look down into my eyes.

"You really want that?"

"More than anything," I say easily. I've wanted this for a long time, but something always held me back from actually asking for it. "Please," I ask again.

He takes in a shaky breath, and for a moment, I think he's going to tell me no. Maybe he's not into anal. I know we haven't really talked about it. My mind is spinning before he lowers his mouth to my ear. "I've thought about what it would be like to be inside you for so damn long."

Relief goes through me at the sound of his words. "Are you going to find out? My ass really is spectacular." I waggle my brows at him, trying to lighten the moment because this is heavy.

He chuckles at that and then presses a firm kiss to my lips that leaves my head swimming. "I don't have any lube. Please tell me you thought ahead."

I grin at him, pointing toward my bag. "I'm like a motherfucking Boy Scout."

He grins back at me, and it's so damn pretty. His smile just does it for me. Everything about Ronan just does it for me, if I'm honest. And yes, I know I'm in way over my head here. That the feelings I'm having aren't going to magically go away from the summer and letting him inside me will likely just make it more difficult, but I need this.

It's like a living breathing thing deep inside my soul. I have to give myself this. I need him to have this part of me.

He climbs off the bed after giving me another bone-melting kiss—it's like he can't get enough, and I'm totally okay with that. He grabs the lube and a condom from my bag but doesn't walk back to me yet. He holds the condom up in a silent question.

Do we really need it?

I shake my head before he even opens his mouth. "I trust you."

That seems to be good enough for him because he tosses it back in the bag and only brings the lube back with him. He doesn't open it yet, though, just tosses it on the bed next to my head and climbs back onto my body, his hands holding my face as he kisses me hard.

There are a lot of things I want to say. That I think he's the most impressive human I've ever met. That I'm sorry I was such a fuck-nugget in his class. That I'm so damn happy I met him.

But I don't say any of it out loud. I like to think he hears them though as we kiss and rut together on the bed. His hard cock drags over mine making us both gasp and moan. We're both leaking and hungry for it, but he doesn't rush it.

I'm close to begging him again when he starts to slowly trail kisses down my jaw and neck to my nipples. He takes his time, licking and sucking, making me writhe and moan, my hips bucking upward, desperately seeking some friction on my cock.

But I don't rush him this time. I let him explore every part of my torso with his mouth. "Your body is so fucking crazy."

I laugh, my muscles flexing tight with the motion. "Home gym at my parents' and now one in my building."

I can feel him smiling against my skin before he drags his tongue over the V leading down to my dick, but of course, this smug bastard bypasses the needy flesh. He kisses my thighs all the way down to my calves and then back up, his hands moving to my knees as he lies between my legs, he pushes my knees up, and I widen them, opening myself to him.

"Fuck." He lets out a deep, shaky moan when he stares right at my hole. "Every part of you is perfect."

"Please, Ronan," I beg, even though I'm not sure what I'm asking for, but Ronan seems to.

He doesn't waste any time. Just dives right in. His tongue sweeps over my hole, lighting up so many nerve endings I didn't even know I had as he licks me. He drags his lush tongue over my hole, over and over, softening it to let him inside. His hands are resting on my knees as he eats me out. The sounds he makes are obscene as he licks and sucks on my hole, making me needy and desperate.

My hands go to his hair, but I'm not pulling him away. I'm sweating and panting as I thrust my cock into the air, needing to come. "I'm so close. Holy fuck, I'm so close," I babble. My cock is dripping so much pre-cum, just sliding down my shaft, and I want to touch myself.

I want to come with his mouth devouring my hole, but I want him inside me even more than I want that. "Please, Ronan. Inside me."

He doesn't let up though. He just continues to lick his way inside me. "Goddamn, you taste good," he says, his breath tickling my balls and nearly sending me over.

"Please. I want your dick inside me now." My fingers tighten in his hair, and every single muscle I have is pulled tight. I feel like I could burst, but I need this.

Finally, he reaches for the lube, and I place it in his hand. I watch him apply some on his fingers, and that's when the nerves kick in. Maybe I should tell him I've never bottomed before, but I'm too afraid he won't do it.

I know I want this—crave it. But when his first finger slips inside of me, he stops, his very aware eyes on mine as he watches me. The man misses nothing. "Have you done this before?"

I won't lie to him.

"No, but I want it. I fucking crave it. Please." Damn, how many times have I said *please* to this man? Don't care.

His eyes are dark and stormy with need and lust, but also concern as he watches me. "Would you rather fuck me?"

My cock jerks violently, and yeah okay, that sounds damn good, but no. "No. I mean yes," I quickly say, "I want that so damn badly, but I want you inside me first, Ronan." I keep my eyes on his as I look up at him with determination. "I can't explain it, but I need this."

I watch him battle with himself for several seconds, but then he nods. "Okay, relax for me." He's so damn gentle when he adds one finger, slowly opening me up. It doesn't hurt, my hole already softened from his glorious tongue-fucking. When he adds a second one, I definitely feel the stretch and burn a little more.

By the time he adds a third finger and a lot more lube, the burn is still there, but it's morphed into hot pleasure too. "More. Your dick. Now." I can't use full sentences, but he doesn't seem to mind.

"If you want me to stop, tell me," he says firmly before removing his fingers and making me whine with desperation. His mouth morphs into a cocky, confident grin as he slathers his cock with lube, and then the head is at my entrance.

He looks down at me, one hand on one of my knees, holding me open for him and the other beside my head, bracing his weight. I think he wants to say something. Stupid hope races through my mind at the prospect of what he wants to say, but then he only leans forward and kisses me as he slowly starts to push inside.

And okay, his fingers are nowhere near as big as his dick, and it

NICOLE DYKES

hurts, but I listen to him and breathe through it. I relax my body as much as I can and focus on the fact that this is Ronan.

That he's making me his in a way that I've never allowed anyone else to do.

And when he's finally inside me all the way, I'm pleading with him to move. But he stays frozen, his cock filling me, stretching me as his forehead meets mine, and we just breathe together.

"You're going to wreck me."

I'm confused for a moment because I'm pretty sure it's his massive cock that's going to wreck *me*, but then I realize that's not what he's talking about.

Not at all.

RONAN

Being inside Fletcher is unlike anything I've ever experienced, and I don't think it really has that much to do with the tight heat wrapped around my cock or his beautiful body underneath mine.

I mean, that's part of it, yes, but the connection I feel . . . it's unmatched.

And I'm never coming back from this. I know it deep down. I'll never be the same.

"I need you to move. I'm dying here," he says, his hands gripping my biceps, a line of sweat formed on his forehead, making it slippery when I move my head from side to side in a slow motion.

I pull away from his forehead and look down into his eyes. "You feel so damn good."

There's that playful, cocky smile I'm used to. Just peering up at me with mirth. I fucking love it. I love everything about him.

I love . . .

That hollow, numb feeling starts to threaten, but I push it away along with any rogue thoughts. Talking about my past, about how hard I worked to get to where I am, should only strengthen my need not to jeopardize my job, but being here with him . . . I think in this moment, I'd give everything up just to be with him.

And that thought is the most terrifying thing that's ever crossed my mind.

You can do this, Ronan. Keep it together.

"Are you okay?" he rasps, and I nod my head, unable to form actual words. I pull back, nearly leaving his body. But then, I push back into him slowly, the chords in my neck pulling tight as I take in every single sensation.

He's warm and tight, strangling my cock as he squeezes around me. "Yes. Just like that."

I move in and out of him slowly, an agonizing pace, but I allow myself to feel every single moment.

"Harder. Don't be gentle with me," he says, his hands moving to my bare ass, squeezing my cheeks and pushing me further into him.

"Oh fuck. You feel so goddamn good. Yes," I breathe and pick up my pace, pounding into him, making sure to hit his prostate with every thrust and making him cry out with overwhelming pleasure.

"Fuck, yes. Holy shit. That. Right there. Do that again."

His nails dig into my flesh, and I feel heat traveling down my spine. "I'm close. So damn close."

"Yes. Come inside me," he groans. And holy fuck, I almost follow his order, my cock jerking inside him, but I manage to keep it at bay for a moment.

I lean down and kiss him hard, panting against his lips, "If you hold out, you can come inside me too."

His eyes widen at that as he looks up at me, his mouth opens, and then he nods his head exuberantly. "Yes. Fuck yes. I want that. Please come. Hurry the hell up."

I chuckle, the move making us both groan in pleasure when he squeezes around me. I push into him only three more times before my cum sprays his insides in the most intense orgasm I've ever had. I call out his name and thrust into him over and over, milking my cock until I nearly collapse.

I can feel his hard dick against my stomach, and I know he didn't come. I smile. "You ready?"

"Fuck yes," he says again, and I gently pull out of him, rolling off his body and getting on my hands and knees. I feel him moving as he gets behind me, his hands going to my ass.

"How disappointed will you be if I come the second I get inside you?" He's joking, but I also hear the nerves there.

"I'll love all two seconds of you being inside me. Now hurry up." I say, bracing my weight on my elbows.

I hear the cap of the lube, and moments later, there's one finger swirling around my hole. He doesn't press inside and for a moment I'm worried he's too overwhelmed. "You think I'm perfect, but I've never in my life seen someone so beautiful."

Goddamn, another part of my heart leaves me in that moment and goes straight to this man.

He uses both hands to spread my cheeks, and I should be totally uncomfortable with him staring at the most intimate part of me, but all I feel is calm.

He gets me ready slowly, and when he's stretched me with two fingers, I'm pleading with him to get inside me. My cock is still spent, hanging half hard between my legs, but this isn't about that.

And when he pushes his way into me, my mind settles, and I just allow myself to feel every second of his big cock stretching my body. I accept him without fail, pushing back against each one of his thrusts.

I didn't plan to come again, but he actually winds up having surprising stamina. And when he pegs my prostate over and over, his fingers digging into my hips as he fucks me without mercy, I cry out at the same time his cum fills my body, coming for the third time in a couple of hours.

He collapses onto my back, and I don't even care that I'm stuck in a puddle of my own cum. "Museums," I say, sounding almost drunk, the word barely audible.

"What?" He sounds amused as he slips out of me and rolls beside me on his back.

"They were my safe space, like libraries are for you. I worked cleaning one of the offices of one for a little bit. They let me enter for free whenever I wanted to. I could stay there for hours."

And I did. For a long damn time, every chance I got, I'd hop on the bus and go to a museum.

I roll to my back and lift my arm for him to cuddle up next to me, his head on my chest. "I like museums too, but I also like to be able to stay still. Just sit in one spot and read."

I kiss his sweaty forehead. "I always had the need to constantly be moving. I spent so many hours at each exhibit, Studying every aspect."

He looks up at me with wide, beautiful eyes, and I swear he's going to say something. Something that's been on my mind. Something I won't allow myself to say. My heart is pounding in my chest with anticipation. *Do I want him to say it?*

Could I say it back?

Would I freak the hell out and ruin everything?

I'm panicking, and I don't know if he can sense it or what, but he just smacks a quick kiss onto my lips and then climbs off the bed in all his naked glory. "I'm starving. We should make dinner."

I don't know if I feel relieved or disappointed, probably a bit of both, but I force myself to climb off the bed anyway, and the laugh that leaves my mouth is genuine when I see the clock. "It's not even four o'clock."

"Yeah well, you fucked me good. What can I say? I'm starving."

I laugh at that and shake my head before I take his hand and lead him into the bathroom. "Shower first. Then I'll feed you."

"Sounds like a plan." He's smiling, but I'm a little worried it's a front. He's really good at doing that, and I don't want him to ever feel like he has to with me.

But at the same time, I'm not sure I can take anything else at the moment.

So maybe I'm a little grateful for that damn "nothing can touch me" smile of his.

FLETCHER

"If I could wake up every single day like this, that would be great," I say breathlessly as Ronan works me over, his mouth hoovering my dick, slowly milking the cum from me as my orgasm starts to fade.

I pull him up to me when my dick gets too sensitive, and he kisses me with that fierce passion I love so damn much.

After we cleaned up yesterday, we grilled steaks outside and had dinner on the patio overlooking the lake. We didn't really let our conversation get too heavy, but we didn't really need to.

He's let me in.

And I don't sense him freaking out about it, which I have to say is an even bigger surprise than him letting me in. But there's a quiet sort of peace there. He let me take him again when we climbed into the bed last night. I finished inside him as I jerked him off, letting his cum spray everywhere as he clenched around me, making me see stars, and then we passed out, cuddled up under the covers together until I awoke to soft kisses on my arms and chest.

I can feel him stroking his hard cock as we kiss, and I want to help him out, but my arms are jelly. He doesn't seem to need it, though, he's doing just fine, and when his warm cum splashes against my stomach, he only kisses me hard as he cries out into my mouth.

We both take a moment to come down from the high and then take a shower together. If I could take all my future showers with him, I think I would. The way he washes me so gently, taking his time to make me feel so damn wanted—it's addicting.

Every single part of him is addicting.

After we get dressed—and once again Ronan is wearing shorts and a t-shirt instead of a stuffy suit—we make a quick breakfast, and then we go for a walk around the lake. It's beautiful here. There's no denying it. There are plentiful trees, which are still green and leafy all around the water's edge.

There are a lot of people here, with it being a big spot for summer vacations. But when Ronan takes my hand in his as we walk, I want to whoop and do a fist pump because oh my God, he's holding my hand out in public.

He didn't have to. I didn't ask him to. He just did it.

My heart does somersaults, but I try my best to keep my cool. I do not want to spook him. By the time we get back to the cabin, we're both pretty sweaty because it's hot as hell outside and so damn humid.

Ah, summer in the Midwest.

"We should go swimming," I say, looking out at the lake. "Did you bring your trunks?"

He smiles. "You know I did. You practically packed for me."

"And aren't you glad I did?" I ask as I race inside, and he follows me. We quickly strip out of our clothes, and okay, I get pretty damn distracted by his body, but he doesn't let me explore.

He pulls on his trunks and shoots me an incredulous look. "Come on. This was your idea."

I'm still totally naked, just hanging onto my trunks, but not hiding my dick—which is up and ready to play after that quick strip show he just gave me. "That was a stupid idea. Let's stay in."

He laughs and makes his way over to me, his hands going to my hips, but he's not looking at my dick. Nope. He's looking right into my eyes. *Damn it.* "Let's go swimming. We need to get the whole experience."

"Fine," I groan, but I'm teasing him. I don't need sex right now. I just need him. Which is scary as hell, but I'm trying to convince myself to live in the moment.

I pull on my trunks, and we head out to the swim beach. There are a lot of people around, but there might as well not be because I don't see them. All I see is Ronan as we splash around in the warm water.

"Damn, this is weird. Muddy," he says, and I can't help but laugh.

"Have you never been swimming in a lake before?"

He looks grossed out, but he's trying. I can appreciate that. "No. I'm a city boy, through and through." I smile. "I prefer to see the bottom of what I'm swimming in."

I laugh. "Well we'll have to use the pool at my apartment sometime."

He grins and shakes his head. "Of course you have a pool." But he's not disapproving when he says it. It's more like he's amused. I think about how hard he's worked to get to where he is.

How he likely had to watch so many rich students come through who didn't have to work. How he thought that's how I was too.

"How do you do it?"

"Do what?" he asks, still pretty focused on the sandy, muddy bottom of the lake we're walking on as we wade into the water.

"Be around all those rich spoiled kids at college? I hated high school. It seemed like everyone had money and attitude."

He seems to think about that now, instead of focusing on the mud. "Some students drive me crazier than others," he says with a grin.

I cackle at that. "Yeah. I'm glad you didn't kick me out of your class. I'd have deserved it."

"No, you wouldn't have," he says very matter-of-factly. "You made me realize how judgmental I've been over the years. There was more to your story, and I should have given you some grace."

"I can't imagine what you've been through."

He gives me a shy smile. "Yes, you can. You lived through it too."

That same guilt I always feel comes creeping up again. "Was it bad?"

The water is up to our chests now, and we stop, just kind of letting it take us, soft waves all around. "Not really. Most of the time,

I was just invisible and lonely. I used to think my mom would come back."

I move a little closer to him, my hand on his side, needing the physical contact. "I would have saved you."

He leans closer to me, his mouth close and his eyes on mine. "I think you did."

I'm surprised by his words, but he doesn't give me the chance to argue with him. His lips press against mine in a firm kiss that's somehow so full of passion, even though it only lasts a second.

I'm so far gone for this man.

And I'm in deep, deep trouble.

RONAN

I really don't want to go back tomorrow.

What the hell is happening to me? I know I ask this a lot, but I can't figure out the answer. I mean, I know it's Fletcher, but I never saw this coming. I promised myself a long time ago I wouldn't ever rely on another person for my own happiness.

That I'd make my own way and not worry about anyone else.

But here I am, walking hand-and-hand with Fletcher after getting back from a restaurant in town where we ate dinner. It's been all sex and fun since we got here, but it's been more than that too.

We've talked about so much. I've really, truly let him in. I'm losing this battle, and it terrifies me because I don't think I can give up my career. My security.

What would that sad, lonely little boy think as he sat there waiting for his mother, begging her to love him enough to come back. What would he think of the older version of himself, giving it all up for . . . for what? I don't know.

It can't last.

I can't betray my younger self.

"You okay?" Fletcher asks me, and I realize I haven't said anything for a bit.

"Yeah."

He stops walking and faces me, still holding my hand. "You sure? Because I can't wait to get my hands on you as soon as we get inside."

I grin. "You're insatiable."

He kisses the tip of my nose and is smiling his actual real smile. "You make me that way. I blame your dick."

I chuckle at his ridiculousness. "Well let's go inside, and you can decide how to punish me for it."

"Oh, hell yes," he says far too excitedly, tugging on my hand until we get up to the door. He unlocks it, and we go inside, barely closing the door before our mouths are fused together. My back hits the wall, and I grunt into his mouth, but I flip it so he's the one pressed against the wall until I hear a quiet grunt and a clearing of a throat.

Fletcher pulls away from me, and we both look over to see a large, tattooed man without a shirt on, but he's wearing jeans. He's staring at us with cold eyes, and my first instinct is to protect Fletcher, my body going in front of his, my arm blocking him.

"Rhys," Fletcher says, the shock evident, but he seems to know this massive, stoic man.

"I thought about coming out completely naked, but this teddy is just too pretty not to show . . ."

"Mom," Fletcher says, and my eyes widen as a beautiful blonde walks into the living room, wearing nothing but a slinky white teddy. The man—Rhys—who I'm putting together is Fletcher's adoptive father, jumps up from the couch now and grabs what I'm assuming is his t-shirt, sliding it on over his wife's head.

When I drop my arm and look at Fletcher, he looks absolutely mortified, shielding his eyes with his hand. "Fletcher. What are you doing here?" his mother asks.

"Are you still naked?" He doesn't drop his hand from his eyes.

"I wasn't naked. Jesus," his mother says, her small body now swamped by her husband's t-shirt as she approaches me. "But I'm covered. What are you doing here?" She looks at me with a kind, amused smile. "And who's your friend?"

"Think they're more than friends," Rhys says.

The woman—Blair, that's her name—her eyes just absolutely light up now. "Oh my God. You have a boyfriend, Fletcher? Why didn't you tell me?"

Fletcher finally looks at his mother but seems awfully wary. "That I'm with a man? Or that I have a boyfriend?" I try like hell not to react to him calling me his boyfriend. I don't say it's just for summer.

I want to blame the shock of walking in on his parents obviously about to get down and dirty, but I don't think that's it. I like the sound of the title. *Fuck. Me.*

"Well, all of it. But do you really think I care that it's a man and not a woman you've snuck off with?"

Fletcher watches her closely, and I'm guessing he's not out to her yet. Or he wasn't. But I also get the impression it doesn't matter to this woman. "No. But I'm . . . I mean I was always with girls."

I frown at that because . . . stupid Josh.

He must pick up on it because his eyes widen. "Oh I guess there was one other guy too."

Blair just laughs lightly and waves him off. "Well, I don't really need a rundown of all of your hookups sweetie, but this seems pretty serious." She looks between the two of us. "I mean, you brought him to the lake house."

He looks slightly pale now, like he doesn't know what to say. And I know it's because he doesn't want to scare me. "I'm a professor," I blurt out, and it gets everyone in the room's attention.

"You're the professor who hates him," Blair says, and wow. Okay, I see the mama bear there, and I'm a little—okay, very—intimidated by the petite blonde.

"Blair." Her husband's tone is calm but firm.

She places a hand on her hip and looks directly at me. "I'm hoping you don't still hate him."

"No. I never did," I say honestly. "I just . . . we just . . ." I'm a stuttering fool right now, and that never happens to me. But damn. I think she might claw my eyes out at any minute. "I didn't know . . ."

"Mom, stop. He had his reasons." Fletcher moves to stand directly beside me. "I'm sorry I didn't tell you about this. It's just he's a professor, and I'm, well, I'm not a student right now." He just had to say that.

I roll my eyes, but I can't stop the smile on my face. "He's a student. I could lose my job. I *should* lose my job," I say, the statement paining me, but it's the truth. I'm sleeping with a student.

"Why's that?" she asks, and she sounds truly confused with her head cocked to the side.

"Because he's a student, and I'm a professor. I crossed a line."

She studies me closely and then looks over at Fletcher. "Did you ever feel like you had to sleep with him, Fletcher? Did you feel like you couldn't say no?"

"Hell no," Fletcher says immediately. "I wanted every single second with him from the beginning. If anything, I seduced the hell out of *him*."

His father groans. "Not something a dad needs to know."

His mother, however, looks oddly proud. Her pretty eyes meet mine. "My son doesn't do anything he doesn't want to do. And lord knows he didn't sleep with you for grades. He has no trouble in school. If he slept with you, it was because he wanted to."

"I did," Fletcher says, and my neck heats.

"It's not really that simple," I say because it's just not. It's black and white. If anyone finds out about this, I'll be fired. The rules are there for a reason.

"It is," she says, and yeah, she did say it quite simply. "Are you two in love?"

"Mom . . ." It's Fletcher's turn to groan.

"What?" She looks at her son, and I almost laugh because she just does not back down.

But then Fletcher speaks, and that darkness starts to bubble up again. "It's just a summer thing."

My heart actually aches in my chest at his words. They're my words. Words I've made sure to say over and over again, but man, do they hurt. Blair frowns deeply at that, and I want to run, but I stay there as she looks at me with extreme disapproval. "Is that so?"

"Yes," Fletcher answers, even though I think she was asking me. "I'm eighteen, and I know what I'm doing."

She turns to look at him, but it's him now who doesn't back down. She's quiet for so long, I start to fidget, but then finally she sighs softly. "Okay, sweetie. You're right." She turns to her husband. "We should go get a hotel room."

"Oh no. You don't have to do that," I say, feeling like a total heel, taking them away from their trip.

She waves me off. "The things I have planned, I can't do with my son under the same roof."

"Mom, God." Fletcher covers his ears. "My ears are bleeding."

She cackles at that as her husband goes to their room, coming back with a new shirt on and sandals for Blair. He slings a bag over his large shoulder and pats Fletcher on the shoulder. "You need anything, and I mean anything at all, you call."

Fletcher nods, not goofing around at all as he agrees, "I will."

Rhys gives me a quick nod before he heads out of the house, and Blair pulls Fletcher into her arms. "I love you, kiddo. I'll be popping in at your place soon."

"Maybe knock first," he says, and his mom laughs, her eyes trailing to me before they settle back on Fletcher.

"Okay. Fine." She smiles and kisses his cheek. "Love you."

"Love you too," he says easily.

She then turns to me, and again, I'm way too nervous. "It's nice to meet you . . ."

I realize she's waiting for my name. "Oh, um . . ." *Great job there, Ronan.* Way to show some confidence. "Ronan."

She smiles and then gives me a brief hug. "Nice to meet you, Ronan. Don't hurt my boy, or I'll bury you."

"Mom," Fletcher groans. "She's kidding," he says to me.

"I'm not," she says with a wink and a smile, a chill going through me because I know she's not. But also, I can't help loving that Fletcher has this woman in his life. Someone who will do anything for him, no matter what.

She's his mother, through and through. And isn't that just goddamn beautiful?

I'm in awe of her as she says her goodbyes and leaves, closing the door behind her.

"I'm so damn sorry. I swear I had no idea they were going to be here this weekend. They never travel. And I was going to text Grayson to ask, but I guess I forgot. Shit. I'm so fucking so—"

I cut him off by kissing those pouty lips of his. He grunts in surprise, but then he comes back from it and kisses me back with vigor. He walks over to the door, flicking the lock, and then he's back on me, our clothes flying off.

I need him so damn badly, I'm salivating for it as we make our way to the couch. I sit down once I'm fully naked, and when he kicks his shorts away, leaving him nude, he straddles my thighs and kisses down my neck. "I'm sorry."

"Don't be," I breathe, stealing his lips again.

"Lube. We need lube," he pants as his hand wraps around my hard shaft, and he strokes me. "Fuck, why is it so damn far away."

"You know . . ." I start. "It occurs to me just now that your parents were probably about to—"

"Oh, hell no." He jumps up off my lap so fast, he nearly stumbles. "Fuck. I'm never sitting on this couch again."

I grin and stand up, reaching my hand out for his, and he takes it, letting me lead him back to the bedroom.

We grab the lube and move to the bed, and I waste no time preparing myself to take him because I'm feeling this desperate need to have him inside me. But he grabs the lube, and instead of getting his dick nice and slick, I watch as he slides two fingers into himself.

"Oh fuck, I need to be inside you, but I need you inside me too. I need you to fill me up with your cum, and I want to feel you for days." I watch him work lube into his hole as he lies on his back on the bed next to me.

"Jesus. Fuck." I nearly come from listening to him. I hurry to get myself ready and then add more lube to my hand, slicking his cock for him and pulling him to me. He doesn't fight me on it, and he doesn't waste any more time. He slips inside my body with ease. "Yes."

"God, I'm never going to tire of this," he says against my lips as he thrusts inside me. He nails my prostate on the first try, and I cry out, loving the way he fills me.

I won't either.

I think it, but I don't say it out loud. He doesn't seem to mind or notice, too lost in pleasure, and it doesn't take long before he's filling my ass with his cum. When he fills me, I nearly lose it but remember his need to have me inside *him*, so I manage to hold off.

He wastes no time pulling from my body, then positioning my very hard dick at his hole. His body accepts me as he slides down over my shaft, and I gasp when I bottom out. The sensation is nearly too great. His hand slides down my chest as he rides me.

I try to hold out even longer, not ready for this to end, but I quickly lose the battle, my orgasm taking hold, and I release into his tight body before he collapses onto my chest, my dick still inside him as my cum starts to leak from him.

I know we have to go back tomorrow.

And I know the summer is going to go fast.

But there's a huge part of me that thinks I could stay here forever.

With him.

FLETCHER

We're back. I wish we could have stayed at the lake house forever, but I know that's totally unrealistic. We got back yesterday, and today, Ronan is back at work. Turns out, Annie didn't need my help today after all, so here I am at my place doing absolutely nothing.

I'm trying really hard not to think about how many days we have until summer is over. I still can't believe my parents showed up at the house. I also thank God we got back to the house when we did, and not a minute later, because I'm pretty sure I'd have had to bleach my eyeballs, and that wouldn't have been fun.

I'm also surprised my mom hasn't been blowing up my phone, but I suspect that has a lot to do with Rhys. He seems to be able to keep my mom fairly calm, but I don't think it will last long.

A laugh jumps from me when I hear a knock on my door a moment after that thought. Okay, so not long at all. But when I go to open the door, it's not Blair, it's Bree standing there. "Hey, Fletch."

"Mom send you?" I ask with one eyebrow cocked.

She tosses her head back and laughs. "Of course. Did you really almost witness . . ." She shudders, and I gag.

"Yes. But never mention that again."

She laughs and holds up her hand. "Promise. Can I come in."

I move out of the way, and she walks into my place, making herself comfortable on the couch while I close the door. I join her and just wait for her to speak.

"So are you in love with him?"

Damn, Bree. "I'm . . ." flustered as fuck. "No. It's a summer fling. It's not a big deal."

"Blair thinks she saw some pretty damn real feelings between you two. And she thinks you're acting all tough."

"I *am* tough," I say, but yeah, it's not convincing at all.

"I know, buddy," she says and pats my shoulder. I roll my eyes, but I can't help but laugh.

"I'm trying."

"You don't want it to end with the summer though, right?" she asks, not missing a damn thing.

"No. But it has to, Bree."

"Why? Because he's a professor at your college? That's stupid," she says bluntly, and I would have agreed, except now I know why his job means so much to him. I can't really tell her the whole story though.

It's not mine to tell.

"Bree." I look into her eyes, pleading with her to get it. "He's like us more than you know. More than I ever realized. He can't lose his job."

Her eyes widen a little, and she seems to think that over. I think she gets it without me having to spell it out, but still she huffs. "It's still stupid. If you like each other . . ." Her eyes bore into mine with no nonsense. "If you love each other,"—I flinch, but she doesn't back down—"you should be together."

"Since when do you believe in fairytales, Bree?"

She grins brightly at me now, settling in to lay her head on my shoulder. "Since we were rescued by the beautiful queen and her sweet king."

That's really damn hard to argue with, so I don't say anything else. I just hang out with her for a while longer before she heads out, and I go over to Ronan's house.

Anticipation and longing thrums through my veins before he

opens the door to let me into his house. The home he built on nothing but determination and hard work.

God, I can't be the reason he loses this.

He pulls open the door, his smile bright, and he's back in his professor clothes with dress slacks and a black button-down shirt. But he still looks hot as all hell. I walk inside, letting him close the door behind me before I wrap my arms around his neck and pull him in for a deep kiss.

"Did you miss me?" He grins when I finally release him.

More than you'll ever know. "Maybe a little." I try to play it cool, and he just laughs as he directs me into the kitchen where he's making dinner. I let myself get a little lost in the fantasy of it all as he cooks, and we talk about our day.

"My sister stopped by today."

"Really?" he asks as we sit down at the table to eat.

"Yeah." I can't help smiling because it's always good to see her. Even if she'd have busted in without telling me she was there, I'd have been really happy to see her.

"Did you have fun?"

I nod my head, pushing the food on my plate around with my fork. "She's worried about me."

"Why?" He looks across the table at me with concern and near panic. "Are you okay? What's wrong?"

I'd laugh at his reaction if it didn't make me so damn sad. Because he truly does care about me. I don't know how we got to this point and how that's true, but it is. And if it weren't for the shitty way he was abandoned and having to pull himself from the hellish upbringing, we might actually have a chance.

Maybe I could quit school.

But I quickly shake that away because I know he'd never allow that to happen. "I'm fine," I say quickly. This man may actually kill me. My heart aches, lying to him, because I'm not fine. Far from it. I want him. Desperately. But I can't have him. "Sisters worry." I put that plastic smile back on my face and play it off the best I can.

"Are you sure?" He's not buying it, but I don't think he actually wants to dig further into it either. I think we're both at the point where we know, but also . . . there's nothing we can do about it.

I'm not sacrificing his job, and he's not going to let me quit school.

So I guess we're just totally fucked.

RONAN

The summer is ending quickly. We only have two more weeks until school starts up again. I try not to think about it. I know I should be preparing to end things with Fletcher. If I was smart, I'd get out now, but I'm apparently not smart at all.

No. I'm at one of my favorite places with Nathan, Annie, and Fletcher, currently watching Fletcher dominate a game of pool with Nathan while I sit in a booth with Annie.

It all feels so damn surreal. So easy in ways my life has never been easy. "Oh my God, could you be any cuter?" Annie exclaims, and I tear my eyes off Fletcher long enough to look at her, seeing she's looking awfully smug.

"What?"

She cackles, then takes a drink of her pink cocktail. "You cannot stop staring at your man. And it's adorable."

I bristle at that. She did not just say that. "What?" I lower my voice and lean a little closer to her from across the table. "What are you talking about? I don't have a man." *And oh shit*, was it that obvious? Did she pick up on something? This is so not good. I swear my eyeballs are sweating.

She looks me dead in the eyes, her gaze her no-nonsense one. "Don't be an idiot."

"What?" I gasp. I quickly look around, suddenly paranoid that someone may hear, but no one is paying attention to us.

Annie raises her eyebrow, like she's waiting for me to calm down, but that's not going to happen.

"You know?" I relent.

"Of course I know." She watches me like I'm totally insane, and I feel pretty damn crazy right now. She knows?

"How are you not totally appalled right now? How are you not lecturing me and telling me to end it right fucking now?" I'm panicking, but when I look around, I still don't see anyone paying any attention to us.

"I'm not appalled because you haven't done anything wrong," she says it so simply I want to scream that of course I've done something wrong. I did something very *wrong* minutes before we left to come meet Annie and Nathan at the bar. I did something *wrong* last night and then fell asleep with Fletcher in my arms. I've been doing something *wrong* all damn summer.

Even if it doesn't feel that way when I'm with him. Even if when I'm with him, it feels the most *right* I've ever felt. I know in my head it's wrong. It has to be. I'm a professor, and he's a student. Black and white. It's wrong.

She just goes on and doesn't wait for me to argue, "I'm not lecturing you because you're a goddamn adult, and so is he." She nods in the direction of Fletcher, but I won't let myself look. "And I'm not telling you to end it because I don't want to see you end it with him."

My mouth drops open in shock, and it takes me a moment to get any words to come out. "You said Professor Tuttle deserved to be fired. Why the hell are you giving me grace here? It's the same thing."

She rolls her eyes at me again. "It's not the same thing. Not even close."

I think about the points Fletcher made about how it's not the same, but to me, on a very basic level, it is. The guilt is gnawing away at me because I know it is. "I'm going to lose my job, and I should."

"No," she says firmly, her eyes on mine. "It was different, and you know it was. Fletcher is different. He's . . ."

"What?" I snap. "He's even younger than the poor kid with Professor Tuttle. Probably even more vulnerable too. He's not what I thought he was. He's not a spoiled little rich boy."

"Fucking duh," Annie says calmly as if she knows that already, and I cock my head to the side in question. "We talk. He's a good kid. I like him a lot, and the fact that you both come from a foster care background isn't a bad thing. It's not a flaw in your relationship, it's a connection. It's powerful. You make each other stronger."

Fletcher told her about his past? "You know about him being in foster care?"

"Yes," she says simply. "I know all about it. About the abuse. The neglect. The fear. God, it was like he was telling me your story through his eyes, Ronan. And you both made it out. You're both strong men."

I stare at her, unblinking and unsure what the hell to say. "I don't have anything to offer him." She starts to argue, and I'm the one to cut her off with a firm shake of my head. "I can't give up my job, and you know I can't. Kids like us, all we want is stability when we grow up. I can't give that up for anyone. I've worked too hard."

Way too damn hard.

Fuck, I think about all the nights I only got one or two hours of sleep because I had to wake up and go to the dining hall on campus, not to eat, but to work before my first class. About cleaning offices and doing so many odd jobs every single day while I went to college.

I never had spring break. I never had summer break. I never had a damn break in my life. I'm only just now starting to breathe, starting to relax. I can't risk my job now that I'm almost fully comfortable.

"You've done nothing wrong." she tries to state again, but it falls on deaf ears.

"I doubt the dean will feel that way."

She shakes her head, and I see the pity she has for me. "You've been happier than I've ever seen you before, Ronan." She looks over at

Fletcher and smiles before her gaze returns to me. "It's because of him. Not your house. Not your job. *Him.*"

I swallow hard, a heavy lump in my throat because I know she's right. He does make me happy. He loosens me up, and I relax when I'm around him. "He makes me happy. But my house and that job— they give me something I've never had in my entire life." I force myself not to look back at him, and I only look at Annie. "Security."

"Is it really worth it without happiness, Ronan?" She's not being rude. She's dead serious. She may be a bit of a romantic, but she has an uncanny way of weighing pros and cons.

"I think happiness is a luxury some of us just never get." I never really thought about being happy when I was a kid. I did, however, think about safety. All the damn time. About having a roof over my head where I knew I would eat that day and I'd be safe at night.

"Oh, Ronan." She sounds like she's in so much pain—pain for me— but she doesn't get a chance to say anything else because Fletcher and Nathan finish their game and rejoin us at the booth.

Fletcher's in a really good mood as he teases Nathan, and we all fall into an easy conversation, like we've been a group of friends for years and not like he's only just joined us.

I can see the affection both of my friends feel for Fletcher. It's written all over their faces as we sit and chat. As I watch him, that same overwhelming feeling I have for him sweeps over me.

I'm in love with him.

There's no doubt about it, and when Annie peers at me from across the table, I know she knows that too. She saw it before I did, and I have no idea what the hell to do with this information.

WE BARELY MAKE it through the door of my house before I'm on him. I may not be able to tell him out loud that I'm in love with him, but I can tell him with my mouth and my hands. With my entire body and soul.

I want to tell him with words too, but I don't have the strength in me to say it out loud and then let him go. It's the last thread. The one thing keeping me together that I haven't actually said the words.

"Oh shit, that feels good," he says as I kiss down his neck and suck hard on the crevice between his neck and his shoulder. "Yes."

When he's this far gone, it's so damn easy to get lost in his raspy, sexy tone. I pull his tank top off over his head and toss it to the ground, quickly following it with my own shirt. I fumble with the buttons, just wanting to rip the damn thing so I can feel his skin on mine, but I manage not to before I toss it behind us. His muscles flex under my fingers as I drag my hands all over his warm skin.

I'm afraid to speak because I'm terrified the words will slip out, so I quickly rid him of his shorts and shoes, leaving him fully naked before me. He's like art. His body is like carved stone perfection.

My eyes run over every single inch of his bare skin, and I drag my hands over his firm biceps, squeezing the muscles and reveling in his strength. His hands are all over me too. Completing the task of getting me naked before his lips slam against mine, and we're kissing as we walk further into my house.

"I need inside you," he says against my mouth, and all I can do is nod because I want that too. Desperately.

I don't want him to move though. This moment is too perfect. I hold up one finger, telling him to wait, and I dash to my room, grabbing the lube and then coming back, giving it to him as I lean over the back of the couch, spreading my legs and pushing my ass out for him.

He makes some sort of strangled noise that goes straight to my dick and makes it even harder than it was before I feel his heat behind me. I feel his hard cock against my ass, sliding in between my crease, but not touching my hole, and his thighs against the back of mine. His front presses to my back as he boxes me in against the couch.

His hands smooth down over my shoulders and my back, his lips making a slow trail down my spine, sending goosebumps through their wake.

"Fletcher," I breathe softly.

"Shh," he says, soothing me. Calming me in a way I've never had. Why does this have to end?

I try to push that thought away and just feel.

I lean into his touch as he grabs the lube and, at an agonizingly slow pace, gets me ready to take him. When he enters me, it's just as slow. Just as reverent. I can't see him as I hold onto the couch, and his pace increases as he slams into me over and over, but I can feel him. I can feel what he's feeling. It isn't just sex. It's not just about getting off.

He's telling me all the things he can't say out loud. And when he nails my prostate as he reaches between my body and the couch, stroking my dick in time with him, I allow myself to really listen to what he's saying before I fall over the edge, and then he lets go at the same time.

He comes deep inside me as his body remains flush with mine. And he pants into my ear over and over again as we both work to come back from the brink.

But I think it's too late.

I'm too far gone, and I'm never going to be able to come back from this.

FLETCHER

School starts tomorrow. I'm all enrolled. Set for my first class at noon tomorrow. But we haven't talked about it. We haven't had the dreaded talk at all. He hasn't brought it up, and neither have I.

I've felt sick to my stomach, just thinking about it. But I can't believe he hasn't brought it up. Instead, we're hanging out at my place, watching a murder doc while eating takeout, and it feels like the most normal damn thing in the entire world.

I don't want to lose this.

My heart pangs with that feeling, but thankfully, before I can blurt that out and get my heart smashed into a million pieces, there's a knock on my door. Ronan turns to look at me, an amused smile playing on his lips. "Your mom?" But then he frowns so deep there's a crease in his forehead, and it's really damn cute. "Or Josh?"

I bark out a laugh. "You jealous?"

His frown only deepens, and oh my God, he couldn't get cuter if he tried. Fuck, I'm so far gone for this man. "Relax." I stand up just as there's another knock on my door a little louder than the first time.

I have a feeling I know who it is even before I hear Rhett's voice. "Open up! You've been ignoring us all damn summer."

"Yeah, you can't get away from us," comes Bree's voice next.

"And we brought food!" *That's Grayson.*

My smile is far too big, and when I look at Ronan, I see a similar one on his face. "Are you going to let them in?" He places his takeout container on the coffee table, looking awfully smug and happy.

That's really not the face of someone who's going to end things tonight, right? Or maybe he's just happy because they'll be here to pick up the pieces when he lets me down gently. *Urgh. He'll probably do it in a way that's smart and calm.*

I won't even know he's breaking up with me until he's leaving. Not that there's anything really to break up. I mean, we aren't in a relationship. I knew what this was from the very beginning, and I told myself I was totally fine with it.

Lies. So many damn lies went into letting myself have this.

"Yeah. I suppose. As long as you're okay with it." I ask him, but he only gently nods at me.

His voice is soft, but firm. "I'd like to meet them."

Before this is over. I add in for him because I can hear the words he didn't say. This is so not good. I walk over to the door on shaky legs and do my best to plaster that big, happy smile on my face before I pull open the door.

"'Bout time," Bree complains, but she's smiling. "You know I'm leaving tomorrow."

Shit. I forgot about Bree flying to New York tomorrow. Jesus Christ, could I be any more selfish? "I know," I lie because yeah, I really did forget.

"Liar," she says, totally calling me on my shit as she breezes past me. Rhett and Grayson follow her with grins on their faces, and they all stop when they see Ronan on my couch.

"Oh, uh . . ." Rhett mumbles awkwardly. "Sorry. Didn't know you had company."

Grayson is grinning far too big as he takes in the man on my couch. "Holy shit. Are you the professor who hates him—but fucked him in front of Blair and Rhys?"

I cringe at that, as does Ronan. "We did not fuck in front of Blair and Rhys." I nudge Grayson's shoulder.

"We were just kissing," Ronan says, a boyish glint in his eyes that I can't stop myself from being infatuated with.

Grayson beams as he walks further into the living room, holding his hand out for Ronan. "Nice to meet you. I'm Grayson."

Ronan stands and shakes his hand. "Ronan. Thanks for letting us stay at your house for that weekend."

Grayson grins. "That place is magic, am I right? I mean, I know what Blair and Rhys were getting up to. They didn't fool me. Rhys wouldn't even look at me."

"Nah. That's just Rhys," Bree says as she approaches Ronan. "I'm Bree. You better not still hate my brother since you're at his place, and I doubt you were all that innocent at the lake house."

"Bree," I groan. She's as bad as Blair.

Ronan, however, just smiles widely at her. "Never claimed to be innocent. It's nice to meet you." He leans in a little closer to her, his eyes full of sincerity. "And I never hated him."

Fuck. I hate the way my stupid heart flutters in my chest. The man just said he didn't hate me. That's all he said. There was no declaration of love, but to my brain, there might as well have been.

Way to guard your heart there, Fletcher.

"I'm Rhett," Rhett introduces himself. Ronan shakes his hand.

"Nice to meet you." Rhett actually smiles at Ronan, which is pretty rare with people he doesn't know, so I'll take that as a win.

"Sorry we busted in," Rhett apologizes, but Bree and Grayson have already made themselves comfortable on the couch. Bree's opening up what looks like tacos from one of my favorite places on the coffee table.

"We brought food though," she says with a waggle of her eyebrows.

"It smells delicious," Ronan says as she hands him one. "Thank you."

She studies him closely, and I don't like it because I know she's analyzing him. Deciding whether he passes the test to be with her brother. Joke's on her—we aren't together. She seems satisfied, though, and grabs a taco for herself. "So what are we watching?"

I shake my head at her, wanting to be annoyed, but I can't seem to bring myself to actually be irritated with any of them. Bree moves to New York tomorrow. I can't believe she's actually going.

But man, am I happy for her. She's been dreaming about this for so damn long. We all had those dreams that kept us going when everything felt so damn bleak, and this was hers.

I sit down between Ronan and her, silently apologizing for the interruption, but I see no irritation on Ronan's face either. He seems totally content to hang out with my family.

Again—why does it have to end?

It's too damn perfect.

And I guess, after all my experiences in life, that's my answer.

RONAN

School has started. And Fletcher is in my classroom right now, giving me those flirty little looks. He shouldn't be in here. We shouldn't be this close at all. It doesn't matter that he's not enrolled in one of my classes. I'm still a professor, and he's currently a student.

But I couldn't bring myself to end things last night.

Not after sitting and talking with his siblings. Not after watching murder docs and then switching over to cheesy slasher flicks they seem to really love, even though they mocked it the entire time.

Listening to the way they are together. To their stories. It was enchanting. I think I'm in love with the entire family, and I've only met each of them once. I'm lost and so damn confused about what to do.

I know I need to end it. That if I don't, it won't end well, but I'm terrified to let him go. I don't want to let this feeling go. Not even for the beautiful security my career allows.

"Fletcher . . . this is a bad idea." The door is closed but not locked, and the shade is drawn. But still, it's the first day of classes, and the hallways are flooded with students.

"I just wanted to tell you to have fun today. Even though I won't be in your class."

I smile at that. Look how far we've come. "Whatever will I do without you coming in late and being disruptive?"

"You loved it," he says, his face so damn close to mine. God, I want to kiss him. I want to kiss him and never stop kissing him.

I love you.

The words ring in my head over and over. I want to say them. I barely hold them in as I breathe in his clean scent and look at his intoxicating grin.

"Okay, fine. I guess I should get to class," he says, his eyes bright, and maybe this will be okay. He has what—three years left as a student. We could do this. No big deal. We haven't been caught yet.

I'm not ready to let him go.

He leans in, and I go ahead and do the same, letting my lips briefly touch his, but it's not enough. It's never enough with him. Damn it.

The kiss intensifies more quickly than I mean for it to, but I don't release him. His hand goes to the back of my hair and clenches tight, holding me there, but then my entire world starts to spin, and I nearly collapse when I hear a deep voice behind me.

"What is going on here?" *Dean. It's the dean. Shit. Shit. Shit.*

I can't move, but Fletcher is fast and pulls out of my hold. His wide eyes meet mine first and then the dean's. *My boss. This is so not happening. It can't be happening.*

How could we be so damn stupid and careless?

"I um . . ." Fletcher looks so damn lost and scared. I want to say something. Anything to make it better, but I'm just stuck. Crippled by my worst nightmare being a reality. "I'm so sorry, Professor Barlowe."

Wait—what? I just stare at him.

He looks over at the Dean. "I'm so damn sorry, sir. That shouldn't have happened. Professor Barlowe was just being kind and directing me to my class. I got a little turned around."

Where the hell is he going with this?

Dean McKay seems to be thinking the same thing. "How did that lead to you kissing?"

Holy shit, the dean of the college saw me kissing a student. There's no denying that's what was happening. *None. I'm so fired.*

"I had a class with him last semester and knew he'd help me," Fletcher starts, and I just stand there, stunned stupid and silent. "But I also sort of had like a little crush on him." My eyes widen in his direction, and I shake my head, but he just barrels on, only looking over at the dean. "I guess when he was so nice to me today, I decided to shoot my shot, but he was about to push me away just as you entered. It was so damn stupid, and I'm so sorry."

I shake my head again at him, trying to get him to look at me. I don't want him to take the fall for me. That's not okay.

I want to scream that it's a lie. That I kissed him, and I've been doing a hell of a lot more with him all summer. That I had plans to do more with him tonight after school too.

"Is that so?" I hear Dean McKay ask.

"It is," Fletcher says, and I want to both kiss and strangle him at the same time. He cannot do this. "And if you need to suspend me, I understand. I know that was totally out of line, but like I said, it was all me. Professor Barlowe never even gave me any indication that he wanted me, and I know he'd never do that. It was all me."

"No," I say quickly, the thought of him being suspended from college enough to finally light a fire under me and make me speak up. "That's not . . ."

Fletcher's gaze snaps to mine, and he gives me a hard look, telling me to shut up.

"Well, as long as this never happens again, young man. I don't have to tell you that I really could suspend you for this behavior," Dean McKay says. "You should head out of here. Go to class. Do you know where you're going now?"

"It won't ever happen again. It was a mistake." I want to puke. I want to scream, *it wasn't a mistake* as Fletcher nods his head exuberantly. "Uh, yeah. I think so. Um, I'm sorry again, Professor Barlowe." He's not acting. His eyes are pleading with me to realize just how sorry he is, and I know. I'm sorry too. I don't want to let him take the fall for me. But I can't seem to get any more words out before he leaves my classroom, giving me one last longing look before he exits.

My chest hurts from holding my breath as I look at my boss.

"Sorry about that, Ronan. Apparently, you're the hot professor around here. Don't think this is the first time I've heard of a student crushing on you." He pats me roughly on the shoulder, and I wince. Not from the contact but because of his words. I don't want Fletcher compared to other students.

I don't like the dean thinking he's just a silly young boy with a fleeting crush.

That's not what this is. That's not what we are.

"But you can't put yourself in that position, Ronan. You know you can't. What if it would have been anyone else walking in on this? What if someone snagged a video? That could have been very bad for your career. I'd have had to let you go. You know the way we're being watched right now with the Rhonda Tuttle scandal."

Again. I might lose my breakfast. If he only knew the truth, he'd be firing me right now, but he's not. Because of Fletcher.

Because he's selfless and caring and good. He could have lost his education for me. And whether he thinks it's important or not, I can't let him risk his academic future like that. How many foster kids grew up wanting exactly what he has? He may say that's not important, but I know it is. I know he feels guilt because he was rescued, and he doesn't think he had much to do with it, but he got himself to college.

I won't let him lose it.

"I'm sorry. It won't happen again," I say.

"Good. You're special, Ronan. I could sense it the first time we met, and I don't want to lose a good professor like you."

He pats me again, and I grit my teeth as he leaves my classroom. I go to sit down at my desk, running my fingers through my hair as the adrenaline from being caught starts to fade, and I'm left just feeling empty.

It was so stupid to get caught like that. I know better.

Or I thought I did.

But when it comes to Fletcher, I'm learning I'm not really all that damn smart.

And I can't keep risking this.

159

FLETCHER

Stupid. Stupid. Stupid.
How the hell could I be so damn stupid?

I should have forced myself to wait until after school to see him again. I woke up in his arms this morning, for Christ's sake. I had breakfast with him. I could have gone a couple of more hours.

But noooooo. I had to stop by for a damn kiss on the way to class. And of fucking course, the dean of the entire college just happens to stop by and watch me kiss one of his professors like a damn idiot.

This is bad.

I know it's bad. I couldn't focus all damn day. I wanted so badly to go to Ronan. Beg him to tell me it would all be okay, but thankfully, my smarts actually won out on this one, and I didn't go near his office.

The good news is the dean seemed to buy my dumbass explanation. He didn't seem to be wise to anything going on, and since Ronan isn't home yet, I'm assuming he wasn't fired.

But the wait and the anticipation are killing me as I sit out on his front porch, my legs bouncing with nerves.

I can't lose him. I waited all last night for him to tell me it was over, but it never happened. When Bree, Grayson, and Rhett left, his mouth was on me in an instant. We went back to my bedroom where we made love in my bed, and then he held me all night long until the alarm went off.

It's going to be okay. We're going to figure it out.

I try to keep telling myself that as I watch Ronan pull up in his Lexus, turning his car off and walking up to the front porch, his expression grim. I try not to read too much into it, and I don't say a word until he lets us both into his home and closes the door behind us.

"I'm so sorry, Ron-" My words are cut off by his mouth on mine. Oh, thank God. Relief rushes through me as I cling to him and kiss him back with all I have. *It's going to be okay.*

He grips my shoulders, and I think he's going to lead me back to his bedroom, but instead he's moving me back, our mouths and bodies separating. "Fletcher."

No. I can hear the pain in his voice. *No.* "Ronan, I am so damn sorry. It will never ever happen again. I won't step foot in your office or your classroom ever again. Okay? I promise." I barely recognize my own voice, but I don't care. I'm as shaky and desperate as I sound. "I feel so awful. I promised you it would be okay. That we wouldn't get caught, and then I did something so damn stupid. And I'm so damn sorry."

"It's okay, Fletcher." But it's not. I can tell by his tone. *Nothing is okay.*

"Nothing even happened. I mean, Dean McKay just thinks I'm a nutjob who kissed a professor for helping me out with directions. Like, it's fine." I'm not sure who the hell I'm trying to convince.

"It could have been really bad though. We were caught, whether the dean realized what he was walking in on or not, Fletcher. We were caught."

"No." I shake my head as he releases me from his hold and takes a step away from me. The foot between us may as well be a mile. "I'm so sorry, Ronan."

"I know you are, baby." My heart pings at the endearment. Shatters right then and there. He looks like he wants to come closer to me, but he's staying where he is. The veins in his neck are popped out like it's taking everything he has to stay still. "I am too."

I shake my head, silently pleading for this all to just be a bad dream. I can't lose him. Never in a million years did I see this coming. I wasn't looking for love at all, but I sure as hell found it.

"We knew it had to end sometime." His voice is strained. There's no conviction in his words.

"No," I say again, the only word I can seem to get out.

"This was just a reminder that we needed to end it, Fletcher. It was a push to do the right thing and end it before anyone gets really hurt."

I'm hurt. I'm aching. I can't stand the pain going through me right now as I look at him and see that his eyes are wet. The tears haven't fallen, but they're there. He doesn't want this to end either.

But he's still pushing me away. "We can . . ." I try, but I have no actual plan.

"We can't," he says as he steps closer to me now, and I nearly weep when he wraps his strong arms around me. "I can't."

And I know he can't. I know it pains him to let me go, but at the end of the day, it's his career that means the most to him. It's his safety and his security. Having this roof over his head.

This is what he needs. And I nearly made him lose it.

I let him hold me. Because I know exactly what this is. *This is goodbye.* His voice rasps in my ear as a single tear falls from my eye and runs down my cheek. "If I could give it up for anyone, it would be you."

I know exactly what this is, and I don't let him go as another tear falls.

"Fletcher, I just can't." And then I feel a tear that isn't my own hit my shoulder, and I close my eyes tight, trying to make my way through the pain.

Nothing has ever been this painful in my life though. Not my parents failing me. Not knowing that I was on my own. Not the hunger or the neglect or the abuse as I went from house to house where I never fit in. Not the cruel words and empty promises.

None of it sliced through me like this moment.

Because I let myself fall in love with him, despite him telling me from the very beginning it would need to end. I fell anyway, and I fell hard.

"We can figure this out," I plead.

"I'm sorry, Fletcher. I'm so damn sorry," is his reply just as he presses a kiss to my temple, and then he does what I was so afraid he was going to do last night. What I feared all summer long.

He lets me go.

RONAN

I'm watching the door again.

I can't seem to stop that habit. I know Fletcher isn't going to walk through the door of my classroom. That after last week, I have effectively totally pushed him away. That I likely won't see him again for a while, and if I do, it will be a fleeting moment.

I didn't want to hurt him.

I'd convinced myself that I wouldn't, but as I held him in my home while we both cried as we said goodbye, I knew I was a fool. That I had ended up hurting us both with my stupid decisions.

I knew better, and for the first time in a really long damn time, I ignored all my instincts. And now look at where we are. When someone does walk through the door of my classroom, it's not Fletcher. It's Annie, and she's looking at me with so much damn pity, it makes me want to throw up.

But I can't really garner the energy to tell her to quit it. "What?"

"Jesus," she says, probably surprised by my rude greeting, but again, I can't seem to find the energy for basic manners. "You look like shit."

"Wow." I glare at her. "You really came here to tell me that? Thanks so damn much." I didn't tell her or Nathan what happened. I haven't

164

talked about anything really with anyone since Fletcher left my house almost a week ago. Since I let him go. I couldn't bring myself to talk about it.

It makes it far too real.

But I know it's real, and I know Annie is right—I do look like shit. I feel like shit. I've barely managed to get myself up, showered, and dressed this last week. I'm pretty sure I forgot to eat today, and I even forgot coffee.

It doesn't really matter. Nothing really matters. It feels like I'm missing an entire part of myself. And how the hell did I get here? I promised myself I'd never ever rely on another human for my happiness. That I wasn't going to be one of those pathetic people who needs another human to feel whole.

And now, here I am. Just looking like shit in my classroom, waiting for the next class to start over and over again until I die. Dramatic? Yes. True? Also yes.

"I'm a really good friend. That's why I'm here." She sits down in one of the desks in the lecture hall in the front row. "Fletcher looks great."

My gaze shoots to hers. "He does?" I mean, he's young. Of course he bounced back. I might have too if I was still eighteen.

"Yup. Handsome and smiley as ever. Flirts with everyone in my class—not in a sexual way—but in that charming way he has about him. Pretty sure at least half my students are totally in love with him."

I absently rub over my heart as it beats painfully in my chest. "That's good."

"No. It's not."

"What?" I ask her exasperatedly. "What do you mean it's not good?"

"It's all bullshit, Ronan. He's back to that fake as hell fuckboy act, and I hate it. I don't know what happened between you two, but I know that something happened. The boy is miserable, and so are you."

Her words sting, hitting me straight in the heart. Fletcher has gone back to his crutch of putting on that bright and shiny act, where no one takes him seriously. And it's because of me. "The dean caught us last week."

Her eyes go huge. "Oh my God. Were you fucking?"

"Annie," I scold. "No. Of course not. It was just a kiss. A brief kiss, but it was in here, and it was beyond stupid."

"But you still have your job," she says it almost like a question.

"Fletcher took the fall." I feel sick to my stomach just thinking about it. Why did I let him do that? "He told the dean that it was all him. That he kissed me and it wouldn't happen again."

Annie seems to take this information in, listening quietly. "Okay. So what's the problem? Sounds to me like you're home free."

I scoff loudly at that. "Are you insane? We aren't home free. We were caught, and it could have been so much worse."

"But it wasn't."

"But it could have been," I argue. "We got careless. I could have been fired. And I swear I've seen McKay around here more and more. He's watching me."

"So quit."

I stare at her in shock. There's no way she just said that to me. "Are you crazy? I'm not giving up my job."

"You're not happy," she points out the obvious.

No. But I have a job. I'm safe.

"I'm sure you could find another job, Ronan." Oh yeah, I'm sure after they find out I fuck students, colleges will be flocking to me with the job offers. This would ruin me.

"It's not an option, Annie."

"You're really just going to let him go?" She stands up from the desk now and makes her way to where I'm sitting. "You're going to give up your real chance of happiness for a job. Because that's all this is, Ronan. You may like economics, and you may even love teaching, but at the end of the day, it's just a job. It's a place. A place that will have no problem replacing you if you left tomorrow."

"It's not just a job though." My throat is raw as I look up at her and beg her to understand. "I promised myself I'd never be that sad kid ever again. That I'd work my ass off, and I'd get my house. I'd get safety and security and it would all be okay because it wouldn't be up to anyone else but me."

She places a hand on my shoulder, squeezing it gently. "Ronan, I know. Believe me, I know. You are one of the most impressive humans I've ever met. I know how hard you worked to get here, and I know how important it is to you. But I promise you, you can have it all. You just have to let yourself try."

"I did try." I look away from her and toward the door, but no one is there. "It blew up in my face. I hurt him. I hurt me. I almost lost my job. How exactly can I have it all? You tell me."

She just sighs softly and squeezes my shoulder again. "I don't want this for you. I want to see you happy. He makes you happy."

I look down at my desk now, hanging my head. "Please just drop it."

My voice is quiet and not stern. I'm begging her because I'm not strong enough for this. I can't talk about it. I don't want to think about it.

"Okay, Ronan."

She takes pity on me, and all I can think is, *Thank God.*

But it doesn't matter if she talks about Fletcher or not.

He's the only thing on my mind.

FLETCHER

"Oh, come on, Fletcher. You know you want to go." Some big jock type whose name I can't remember nudges my shoulder as we walk through the middle of campus. He's trying to get me to go to a party at his frat house tonight.

I've been back in school for almost two weeks now, and I've already made friends.

Yay me.

"Nah, I don't think so. I'm not really into parties," I tell him truthfully, but I say it with that practiced big bright smile that makes it seem like I don't want to jump off a damn cliff.

And okay, I don't actually. Don't worry. But honestly, deep down inside, everything hurts. I can't stop thinking about Ronan. Wondering if he's okay. If he's as miserable as I am. Annie says he's actually much worse, but I don't think that's true.

If it were, he'd have sat outside my apartment and begged me to take him back, like I've contemplated doing almost every single night since we ended things between us.

Or *he* ended things.

I was prepared to figure this all out. I feel like we could have, but

168

there's something holding him back. Something that's been holding him back from day one with me, and of course, I know what that is.

He can't lose his job. He loves his job. But I don't know. I think it's more than that. I think he loves me too, but he's afraid.

"Aw, man. Are you sure?" He really wants me to go to this party, but it's not happening. Still, I'm not going to crush the guy.

"We'll see. I gotta get going though. I'm starving and have another class in an hour."

We do some weird bro hug thing, and then I dart off, not wanting to waste any more time with this guy. And although I am actually starving, I don't really want to eat. I don't really want to do anything.

I make my way to my apartment. But when I get to the door, I realize it's not locked, even though it was when I went to class. My shoulder sag, and I huff as I push open the door, not at all surprised to see Blair sitting at the counter.

"Still breaking and entering," I say with absolutely no emotion and close the door behind me.

She climbs off the stool, walking over to me with a coffee in one hand and a brown paper bag in the other. I can smell my favorite sub in the bag, and although my stomach growls, there's no joy in it.

"Mickey's. Thank you," I manage, but instead of handing the bag and coffee over, she places them on the counter and then wraps her arms around me.

"Sweetheart."

"I'm okay," I barely choke out around a sob because I'm so not okay.

"No. You aren't," she says instantly and then pulls back, moving her hands to cup my face, and then I realize she's wiping tears from under my eyes. "You didn't get excited about a meatball sub. Something is very, very wrong."

She's also tearing up, but she manages a smile, which makes me smile too, even with tears falling. "He ended it."

She's still holding my face. "Oh, honey. I'm so sorry." She releases my face, but only to wrap her arms around me once again and hold me tight. I don't push her away. I let her hold onto me. I let her comfort me because I'm just so damn tired. I'm exhausted from pretending I'm okay.

I'm not okay.

I'm miserable and sad, and I miss him so damn much, it hurts me every single day. I wanted him. I wanted to work it out, and he pushed me away.

We move over to the couch, and she doesn't bother grabbing the food. Just wraps her arm around me and lets me lean on her shoulder —which probably looks ridiculous, given our sizes, but she doesn't seem bothered, and neither am I.

"He can't lose his job." I can't tell her too much, but I don't think Ronan would mind a little more information going to Blair. Not that I'll ever see him again anyway. "He's like me, Blair. And Rhett and Bree. He needs his job because he never had anything that was his before."

She takes in the information, and I know she knows exactly what I'm saying. "Well, okay. But haven't you two been keeping it a secret? Why would he lose his job if you do that?"

Because I'm an idiot. My throat aches so bad with the pain of the truth that it's hard to speak, but I make myself. "We got caught. Well, sort of. The dean sort of walked in on us kissing in a classroom."

I can feel her amusement, even though I'm not looking at her, and thankfully, she chooses not to tease me about that. "So, he got fired?"

"No," I say as I shake my head. "I told the dean it was all me. That I kissed Ronan for helping me find my next class."

She does let a soft laugh escape this time, but it's very small and brief. "I'm sorry, honey. But wow, he really thinks you're easy, huh? Just giving kisses for directions."

"Mom," I say with a warning.

She clears her throat. "Sorry. Okay." She lets out a rapid breath. "Not funny. Okay, so the dean believed you?"

"He did," I say, but it didn't matter. "It scared the hell out of Ronan though. He ended things, and it's stupid, I shouldn't be upset. I knew it wouldn't last. He told me that when we first started this thing, and I don't know what the hell I was thinking."

"I do," Blair says it with so much confidence, I actually sit up so I can look at her face as she speaks. "You were thinking he'd change his mind."

"I . . ." I start, wanting to argue with that because I wasn't trying to manipulate him or anything, but I guess I was hoping he'd maybe change his mind after we spent time together.

"Of course you were," she says matter-of-factly. "And it worked too. I saw the way he looked at you. He fell just as hard as you did. He's just a stubborn shithead."

I smile at that, but it fades. "He's not in love with me, Blair. He let me go. He told me he couldn't do it. He never said he loves me."

Of course I didn't tell him I'm so desperately in love with him either. But that's really not the point.

"Oh, honey," she says softly as she shakes her head. "I think you're more like me than I ever realized." I'm not so sure about that, but I don't argue with her. "You know I love Rhys more than life, right?"

I nod my head slowly. "Yes." I drag out the word because I'm not really sure where the hell she's going with this.

"Well, he didn't make it easy. I knew I loved him. That we were supposed to be together, but he didn't know how to be loved, Fletcher. He'd been through so much agony in his life. He'd been so abused. So put down." I nod my head solemnly because it's no secret that Rhys's life was hell in foster care too.

He doesn't really talk about what happened to him then, but we all know it was bad. That he can barely stand to be touched, even to this day, and that he's quiet most of the time. But he loves Blair. And he loves us.

That's never been a question, at least not to us.

"He fought me the whole way, and I'd do it all again in a heartbeat. But sometimes, when you have to survive your whole life with never depending on anyone else, love is too hard to believe. It's too hard to let in.

"But I was willing to. It's scary for me too, Blair."

She places a reassuring hand on my cheek. "I know. Believe me, I know. But still, Fletcher, after everything you went through, you have

171

this uncanny ability to let love in. You did with Bree. You did with Rhett. And then, you did with Rhys and me."

"You're my family."

"We are." She smiles. "But it's not so easy for some people to let others in. To give away that sort of control over your life, it's hard. It doesn't mean he doesn't love you. It means he's scared, and maybe you're going to have to push a little."

I shake my head. "I don't want to force him to love me." I laugh humorlessly because the notion is insane. You can't make someone love you.

"Oh no, you can't force someone who doesn't love you to love you. But he does love you. He's scared. And I imagine his job is important to him. I'm guessing he was in foster care too?"

I nod. "But no one saved him," I croak. "He had to do it all on his own. No one came for him."

"Then you save him from himself, Fletcher." Her tone is firm and surprises me.

"I can't."

"Yes, you can." She doesn't back down. "This whole narrative where we must be strong and only take care of ourselves. Never rely on anyone." She waves her hand in a dismissive way. "It's all bullshit. We are supposed to lean on other humans. We're supposed to get love from others. It doesn't make you weak to need love, Fletcher. Love makes you stronger."

"I don't feel very strong right now," I admit.

"You're one of the strongest people I know, Fletcher. You should have been an angry, mean, horrible little man." My eyes widen a little at that because is that what she wanted me to be? She goes on, "But you weren't. Not ever. Not even when you were bruised from another human being's hands—from someone who was supposed to take care of you—not when everyone and the system let you down over and over. No. You were still sweet. Still kind. Still caring. That's strength, Fletcher. When you get beat down over and over again, but you still find it in you to be kind and brighten other people's day. That's the most beautiful kind of strong."

I wipe at my leaking eyes. "You knew my smile was an act?"

She hugs me to her again, wrapping her arms around me as best she can. "Oh, honey, of course. We all knew that. But it doesn't make you fake. You always wanted to be happy. Circumstances just didn't allow it."

"I was really happy with him, Blair."

"I know," she says and hugs me close to her, kissing the top of my head. "What can I do to make it better?"

I smile sadly at that. "I don't think you can this time."

"That simply can't be true," she says, and I laugh because I can feel she's in fix-it mode already.

"Please let it go."

She lets out a soft, watery laugh and kisses my head again. "You're my kid, and you're hurting. That's simply not possible, kiddo."

I can't help smiling into her hold because if anyone could fix it, it'd be Blair.

I just hope she doesn't resort to blackmail and threats.

That would be kind of embarrassing, and I'm pretty sure Ronan is a little afraid of her already.

I mean, we're all a little afraid of Blair.

She's just the right amount of crazy.

Still, I really don't think even Blair can fix this for me. He doesn't want me enough to make it work.

I really need to let it go. Try to find some joy without him. I could probably do it.

Maybe.

Okay.

Maybe not.

RONAN

There's a knock on my door, and since it's Saturday, I haven't even bothered to get dressed yet. I feel like shit, and for the first time in a long time, I just haven't had the energy to get up out of bed before ten in the morning.

Now I'm regretting that, of course, because someone is at my door. Maybe it's just a package. I just lie there in nothing but my boxer briefs under the covers and hope like hell they go away.

But the knock comes again.

Goddammit. If it's Annie, she's for sure going to call me on my bullshit. I don't want to be fixed right now. I did the right thing. I let Fletcher go without wrecking his college career and my actual career.

It was what needed to happen, but that doesn't mean I feel good about it. Not at all. I just want to wallow for a little bit longer.

I'm a grumbling mess as I grab a pair of sweats, hoping they're clean, but I have no idea. I tug them on before grabbing a t-shirt and pulling it on over my head. I realize far too late, that it smells like Fletcher. That it's one he borrowed after one of our many times in bed.

That's just fucking great.

There's another knock, and this one seems less patient. "I'm coming," I grumble as I make my way down the hall to the front door. I don't bother checking who it is before I pull the door open. When I see Fletcher standing there—looking as gorgeous as ever in a t-shirt and jeans since it's a little cool today, his bright white smile nearly blinding me—I'm stunned stupid. "Fletcher?"

"Hey there, Professor." The way he says that makes my entire body heat, familiarity and longing creeping up, but he's not mine anymore. I let him go. What the hell is he doing here?

"What? Why are you . . ." I can't seem to form words, and he looks amused as his grin widens. Damn, he looks good. Far too good. And I look godawful. This should be embarrassing, but I'm too tired to care. It's obvious I've fallen apart since our breakup, and Fletcher is only thriving.

I'm happy for him. God, I just want him to be happy. I want him to have the best damn life, and it seems he's living it. *So why is he here?*

"What's going on?" I finally ask with a full sentence.

"Can I come in? I just want to talk."

My first thought is *yes*. I mean, right away. No hesitation. But finally, my brain kicks in right before I can say anything. "I don't think that's a good idea, Fletcher."

"Please?" He doesn't miss a beat, flashing those big blue eyes at me. And I swear he's even pouting. Who the hell could say no to him?

Not me. "Okay," I relent and move out of the way, so he can walk into my house. He breezes past me, and damn, he smells good. I'm surrounded by Fletcher—his damn scent all over the shirt I'm wearing and him right here in my space as I close the door behind us.

My head is swimming, but I manage to stand there stoically and wait for him to speak. "I want to show you something, and I want you to stay calm and talk to me about it before you freak the hell out." He pulls his phone from his pocket.

"I don't ever freak the hell out," I start to argue, but he raises one thick eyebrow at me to shut me up.

I huff, but I don't say anything else. He holds his phone up to me, and I see it's some sort of acceptance letter.

"What is this?"

175

"It's an acceptance of my transfer to Rockford."

Rockford College is a private college about two hours from here. Oh no. "You didn't do that," I say, surprised as all hell and shaking my head. "Fletcher, tell me you did not quit school for me."

I feel sick to my stomach and actually wrap my arms around my waist to try to hold myself together.

"No. I didn't."

I stare at him, huffing loudly. "This says you did." I point to his phone, and it's his turn to huff at me as he stuffs his phone in his pocket.

"No. It says I put in for a transfer to a different college, which I did. And of course I got accepted. I mean, I still have to finish this semester, but starting next semester, I won't be enrolled in this college any longer."

"You shouldn't have done that for me," I say, shaking my head because who does that? "You can't rearrange your whole life for someone you just met, Fletcher. We've known each other for a year."

"That's all I needed." He steps into me, and even though I know I should step back, I don't move. "That's all the time I needed to know I'm completely and totally in love with you. Hell, I knew it well before a full year of knowing you, but I guess I was too afraid to say it."

I need to fight this. He's young. This is his first taste of love . . . or whatever, and he just doesn't know. "Fletcher, you don't love me," I try.

But he's not having it. His shoulders square, and he stands up even taller, his head held high. "I do. And I'm sorry if that scares you, but it doesn't make it any less true. I'm in love with you, Ronan. No doubts. No fear. I love you."

My heart is pounding rapidly in my chest. My palms are actually sweating. I feel nothing but fear right now. He can't mean that. I shake my head. "You're young."

"Don't do that," he cuts me off right away. "If you don't love me, that's fine, but don't you dare use my age against me. We aren't that far apart in age, and we both know I'm a different type of eighteen. I know what I want."

I shake my head. "You cannot rearrange your life for me simply because you want to keep having sex with me. That's insane."

"Oh, I for sure want to keep having sex with you." His voice drops into a sexy, husky tone as he steps even closer to me and places his hands on my hips, holding me in place. "But that's not all I want, and you know it. Deep down, you know how much I love you. That I want everything with you, not just sex. I want a life with you. I want to come home to a place we call ours, and I want to make dinner together and talk about our day. I want to annoy the shit out of you and watch you roll your eyes at me, but also . . ." One of his hands moves to my mouth, his finger dragging along my lips. "You can't fight smiling because you're not actually that annoyed with me."

"Fletcher," I say weakly. *God, I want all that.* "No one loves me."

He only smiles, and then his hand cups my jaw. "I do."

I shake my head. I want to believe him. But how can I? My own mother didn't love me enough to come back for me. No one after that loved me enough to keep me. It was always on me. I was always alone. I've learned how to be happy being alone. "I . . ." I falter because I don't know what the hell to say.

But Fletcher doesn't seem discouraged at all. "I know, baby," he says so damn easily, I want to melt into him. "I feel it too, you know? The fear that maybe no one will ever really love me. Or I did before Blair came along. It took me a while to feel like someone could love me for real."

"You deserve that," I say, and I mean it more than I've ever meant anything in my life. Fletcher deserves love.

He grins, wide and beautiful. "So do you, and I'm going to show you. I'm sorry I didn't tell you before. I love you more than anything in this world. And I know it's going to be hard for you to believe that, but I'm going to show you, and you're going to let me. You know why?"

I shake my head slowly, his hand still on my face. "Why?"

"Because you deserve love too. You don't see it, and I get it, but I'll show you. I'm just the right kind of stubborn you need. I'm going to love you so damn hard, you'll never question it again."

I let out a sob, wanting so badly to believe him. "I love you too, Fletcher."

God, his entire face lights up at that. "I know you do. But man, is it good to hear it."

I smile and he presses a soft kiss to my lips. "I love you. I love you. I love you," he whispers against my mouth.

"I love you too," I finally say the words I've wanted to tell him for so long, and it's not as terrifying as I thought it would be. "But I can't let you rearrange your whole life for me." Before he can argue with me, I quickly press another quick kiss to his lips. "I'm sorry. I should have talked this out with you. You're right, you aren't immature just because of your age. I should have talked to you."

"You should have," he says smugly and then pulls me over to the couch with him. He plops down and wraps his heavy arm around my shoulder. "Let's talk now."

"You can't sacrifice your education for me," I start.

He just scoffs loudly. "Please. Rockford is costing my parents three times what it costs to go to school here. Clearly, it's the better education."

I can't help laughing at that, but I shake my head too. "So Blair got involved."

"Oh, yeah." He chuckles. "Full mama-bear mode. She had no problem whatsoever with this plan, though, just so you know. Rhys and she are fully on board." He turns his head, and I turn mine so we're looking directly at each other. "There's nothing she won't do for love."

I smile at that, but it fades. "I'm afraid to let you change your world for me, Fletcher."

He just shrugs his wide shoulders. "I want to go to college, that's true. But it never really mattered to me which college. This is the perfect solution. I won't be a student at the college where you teach. At this school, I'm hoping to be just your boyfriend. I'll be a student at Rockford."

I grin and shake my head. "Jesus. Was it always that simple?"

He smiles. "You know it wasn't always just about losing your job, right? I mean, not really."

I nod because yeah, I do. My job is important to me, and I don't want to lose it. It would have wrecked me, but I was scared. Plain and simple. "I couldn't believe someone could love me. Not for real."

He nods. "I know. I know you're terrified to let your happiness hang so much on another human being loving you. It's scary."

"It is."

He grins and kisses me softly. "But you know that ship has sailed already. I hate to tell you this, but I've been ingrained in you since that first kiss."

"And not at all modest about it."

His smile widens. "Nope. You're ingrained in me too. You make me happy."

"Relying on another human to make you happy is dangerous, Fletcher. I'm a grumpy bastard. I don't want to ruin you."

"Then don't," he says simply as he holds onto me. "Love me just as fiercely as I love you. Hold me tight and never let me go. Even when you're scared."

"I *am* scared," I say honestly and then cup his face in my hands and look him straight in the eyes. "But I do love you. Fiercely. Forever. No matter what. I'm so goddamn in love with you, Fletcher."

He smiles and then smashes his lips to mine in a punishing kiss that tells me just how much he loves me too.

I can't believe I almost let fear win. I can't believe I almost lost him because of it. But I know, without a doubt, I'm never letting him go again.

Fletcher is mine to love, and I'm his.

FLETCHER

He's mine. I should have never doubted Blair. And as soon as she came up with the easiest plan in the world for me, I knew I was going to get my man. To some, changing colleges may seem like a big deal, but for me, it was a no-brainer.

"Rockford is two hours from here." Ronan, of course, is overthinking, but I can also feel that he's in this with me.

He loves me.

I can't stop the bigass smile from taking over my face at that thought. That's really all I need.

I knew I couldn't ask him to give up his career or his house. Those were the two deal-breakers for me. But me transferring to another college? That was easy. "It is." I move my body, throwing one leg over his lap, so I'm straddling him on the couch. His hands go automatically to my hips, and I smile. "Why are we still wearing clothes?"

He laughs and leans up to kiss me, but he doesn't let me get lost in the kiss. He's pulling back now to look at me and keeping me at bay. It's been far too long since I've been this close to him. My body is responding to the close proximity, as always, and I can feel his hard cock tenting his sweats and trying to get to me too. But no, my man wants to talk. *Damn it.*

"We need to talk." *See? Ugh, why did I have to fall for someone so damn logical?*

"Fine. Yes, it's two hours from here, but most of my classes are online. The ones that aren't, I blocked together, so I'll only have to go to campus two days a week. I'll go to a couple of classes and then come home." I lean into him, my mouth nuzzling his neck as I place soft kisses there. "Why are we wearing clothes?"

He laughs softly and then his hands go to the hem of my t-shirt, lifting it off my body and tossing it behind us. "That better? Now can we talk?"

I shake my head, frowning as I stare at the offending fabric covering his sexy as fuck torso. "Not even close."

He chuckles again, and damn, if that isn't the best sound I've ever heard. He huffs like he's irritated, but he's smiling far too big for that to be true. I scoot back a little bit, enough for him to remove his shirt, and my hands go straight to the bare skin of his torso. I let my hands smooth over his warm, strong chest. Over every single muscle and the light dusting of hair over his pecs.

"God, I've missed you." I lean forward and place a kiss over his heart.

His eyes flutter closed, but he uses his hands to pull me back, so I'm looking at his face. "I missed you too. But we should talk."

"Why?" I ask with a grin and then wink at him when he gets all flustered. "Okay. What else?"

"You're still a student here until winter break."

I nod, hating that fact, and I'd have dropped out, but I knew for a fact *that* would have been met with resistance. From Ronan and maybe even my parents too. "I am. But I won't go near your classroom or your office until then. And if you want me to stay away from your house, I can do that too." I swallow, trying to make the thick lump that's formed in my throat go away. It doesn't work. "And if we have to cool it until then, I can try."

He gnaws on his bottom lip, and I swear I'm holding my breath now. I can do this. It's only a couple of months. Just knowing he's the prize at the end of it, I could do it. But then, he shakes his head. "No.

God, I think that would kill me. I'm not sure if you can tell, but I haven't been doing so well."

I smile. "Is that a joke from Ronan Barlowe?"

He laughs. "Hey, I joke around sometimes."

"I know, baby," I say in a mocking tone, my hands going back to his naked chest, unable to stop touching him. "You're hilarious."

He rolls his eyes at me. "We can be careful, but I need you. I can't be without you ever again. I don't want to."

My insides are dancing now. I'm so fucking happy to hear that. "Good. Because I was bluffing. I might have ended up hiding in your bushes or something crazy."

"My little stalker," he teases, and then finally, it seems he's done talking. His lips move to mine, and before I know it, we've both ditched the rest of our clothes, and our bodies are writhing and grinding together as we make out on the couch.

His hand wraps around us both as our dicks slide together, using our pre-cum as lube. "Fuck, Ronan. You feel so good," I gasp as I thrust against his hot flesh, and my hands grip his shoulders.

"I missed you so damn much," he says as his grip gets tighter around us as he jacks us. That's music to my ears. I wanted to believe he'd be okay without me, but a part of me wanted him to realize he could be so much happier with me. That we need each other. That we want each other.

Blair is right. We don't have to go through life alone to be tough. Love makes us stronger, and I'm going to show him.

"I'm close," I pant. "God, I want you inside me." My balls are heavy and pulled up tight. I nearly lose it, but my eyes pop open, and I reach between us, stilling his hand. "I need you inside me."

He nods, not arguing as I stand up, reluctantly pulling away from him, my balls revolting because we were so damn close to release.

But we race into the bedroom, me heading straight for the lube. I pour some on my fingers as I toss the bottle to Ronan, way too keyed-up to have any chill. I lie on the bed and spread my legs, eagerly preparing my wanting hole for him. He watches me as he pours lube in his hand and strokes his long, thick dick.

"Yes, God." I tip my head back, my feet planted firmly on the bed and my legs spread. "I need you."

He strokes his cock, the tip red and leaking. I watch as he trembles, seemingly almost going over, just watching me play with my hole.

"Don't you dare come," I command and remove my fingers from myself, wiping them on the bed, then beckoning for Ronan to join me. He comes to me, kneeling between my legs and bending down to steal into my mouth.

I kiss him hard, gripping the back of his head, not wanting even a second away from his mouth, and thankfully, he seems on board because I feel his cockhead at my entrance. He takes his time filling me, and I'm a panting mess by the time he's fully seated.

"Fuck me, Ronan. Make me yours."

"You already were," he says as he moves my legs back and pushes further into me, making me moan. "Mine." He kisses me hard and then pulls back before shoving into me again. "Mine."

"Yes," I pant as I start to stroke my cock as he moves in and out of my hole. Stretching me. Owning me. "Yours."

My thighs shake with the impending orgasm. Each time he nails my prostate, a jolt of pleasure like none other rips through me. And before long, I can't take it anymore before I'm shouting his name and spraying cum everywhere.

He lasts five or so more strokes before he's filling me up with his release, and then he collapses onto my sweaty, well-used body. I drag my hand over the back of his hair as he lies on my chest, and I hold onto him for dear life.

"Thank you for coming back for me, Fletcher."

I smile as I stroke his hair. "I'll always come for you, Ronan. Always."

I can feel him smiling against my skin as he holds onto me, clinging desperately to me like he can't quite believe I'm here.

As if I could ever let him go.

That will never happen.

He's mine, and I'm his. Forever. No matter what.

EPILOGUE

Fletcher
   About four months later...

"Are you sure I look okay?" Ronan is fidgeting with his collar, and it's the cutest damn thing.

"Aw, are you afraid of Blair?" I tease. He doesn't need to worry. She absolutely loves him and was thrilled to find out that he was fully on board with her plan for us. She immediately invited him over for dinner and fussed over him, just like she does with all her kids.

Ronan looks far too serious when he says, "Of course I am. That woman would bury me all by herself. I have no doubt." She wouldn't. He's one of her kids now, but still, this really amuses the hell out of me.

I remove his hands from the collar of his button-down shirt and take them in my hands. I kiss the tip of his nose. "That's only if you hurt me," I say with a menacing grin, and he just glares at me, but then I see the hint of a smile. He knows I'm messing with him.

And I know he isn't going to hurt me. I feel it deep in my soul. Now that he's opened himself up to love, he's all-in. I don't sit around and worry about losing him anymore or him letting me go. There's a peace there now. I know we're solid. That he's it for me, and I'm it for him, no matter how young we are. No matter what, this is it for us.

"Blair is just happy to have all of her babies home for Christmas," I assure him as I knock on the front door of my parent's house. Why I bother knocking, I'm not really sure, but Ronan insisted.

It's been a hell of a ride these past few months since we finally got our shit together. I kept my word and stayed far away from his office —even only helping Annie out by meeting at the library because she knows what's up.

She was more than happy that we finally got it together and are an official couple. I did have to help her out in classes as her TA, but thankfully, I kept my head down and my eyes to myself any time I was even close to Ronan's classrooms.

There was no way I was going to mess this up for him. We kept our distance until my last final—well, on campus anyway—he spent a hell of a lot of time at my apartment during the times we weren't on campus.

But now, I've given up my place and moved in with him. It's bliss. I mean, that's probably cheesy as hell, but I really don't care. I get to wake up every single morning in his arms, and I get to shower with him often. It *is* my absolute definition of bliss.

His dream has become mine. I love our house. We've been making plans to remodel one of the bathrooms and the kitchen. We've talked about extending the backyard patio. We're making it ours.

I'm not worried about attending Rockford at all. It was never about the place for me. He has a life at this college, but I never really set roots down here. All I need in this world is currently under the roof of this house and standing right next to me.

I squeeze Ronan's hand as Blair pulls open the door, looking fabulous as always in black pants and a cashmere sweater. "You're finally here! I was getting worried. About to come drag you both home." She pulls me into a hug and then Ronan, squeezing us both tight and letting us into her home—my home. It will always be my home too.

And now that she's pretty much adopted Ronan—because he's family now too—it's his home also. That's just how Blair is.

"We were doing our best to keep her distracted," Rhett says as he and Grayson greet us as we take off our coats and hang them on the coat rack.

"It wasn't working," Grayson chuckles.

"Hush," Blair says as she cups my face in her small hands. "I just missed you."

I laugh as she presses a quick kiss to my forehead. "I saw you last weekend," I say and smile. "But I missed you too."

"Hey, son," Rhys says as he walks into the foyer. "Ronan." He actually half-smiles at my boyfriend, and I'm taking that as a win.

Ronan greets him, and then Bree comes in to give us both hugs and complain that we aren't eating yet. Max and Ian run past us in a blur toward the dining room, and we follow the chaos that's my family, walking with our hands joined and sitting down next to each other at the table.

We eat the meal Blair had catered, and we laugh and talk about Bree's experience in New York and how I'm transferring schools soon. Grayson and Rhett are talking about adding more to the lake house and how someday, they really want it to be their permanent home.

It's all so very normal.

And then Ian tosses a roll at Max from across the table, and instead of Blair getting mad, this woman . . . she scoops up some mashed potatoes in her spoon and flings it across the table at Ian.

It hits him square in the cheek, and Rhys groans, but he's happily amused. "Really? Can we not have one dinner that doesn't end up on the floor?"

Blair then hits Rhys right in the face with potatoes, and then it's on. Most of our holiday dinner winds up everywhere, but no one is mad. Everyone is laughing like crazy, having a blast and not taking life too seriously.

That's what Blair taught us.

That love makes you stronger and that life isn't that hard or serious, it's what you make of it.

I hold up a roll that's already been buttered and threaten Ronan with it, and he shakes his head at me. "Don't you dare."

"Why? What are you going to do to me if I do it?" I say, waggling my eyebrows.

He laughs and grabs my hips, shaking his head at me. "Don't do it."

"Will you still love me if I do?" I tease.

His face goes completely serious now, his intense eyes on mine. "I'll always love you. No matter what."

I lean in and kiss his lips softly, but then pull back. "Good." I smash the roll onto the top of his head and run, but he catches up with me quickly, catching me, and smashes some potatoes on top of my head. We laugh and kiss as the chaos ensues in the dining room.

I never thought I'd be here. It seemed so dark and lonely when I was a kid. I never thought I'd have happiness like this or anything even close to it.

But because of Blair . . . Because of my family. And because of Ronan, I now know what being blissfully happy means.

It's not easy. It's not supposed to be. You have to fight for what you want in this life, and I'm happier than I've ever been.

I'm not that scared kid anymore, and my smile isn't fake. I don't have to try to convince the world I'm happy.

I just am.

The End

NOTE FROM THE AUTHOR

Thank you so much for reading *Too Hostile*. I hope you enjoyed it as much as I enjoyed writing it. I swear, I've said that so much, but I still mean it. I love writing these stories, and it means so much to me that you all read them.

I still can't believe this is my actual career. You all have made my dreams come true, and I'm forever thankful for that. I wasn't sure I'd ever actually write this book. *Hostile* changed my life. It did so well that I was left in utter shock during release week. I couldn't believe it, so I put a lot of pressure on this book—until I started writing it. And then it was like I was just coming back home.

I love these characters so dang much. They're just part of me now. Blair is the mama we all wish we could have. She's fierce and strong. Loves her kids hard, no matter what, and just goes with the flow. Rhys is strong and the type of man you're happy to have in your corner. And Fletcher . . . Fletcher is proof that you don't have to let the bad world make you cynical.

I know some will be frustrated with Ronan, but I hope you'll give him some grace. People who have to fight for everything they have—it's so easy to become jaded and untrusting. Especially when you don't have someone like Fletcher or Blair to pull you out of it.

But he came around, you all! We can all make it through this world and be truly happy. Don't be afraid to lean on someone when you need to and to be the bright light the world needs.

Thank you so much to my girls and my amazing husband for putting up with my crazy deadlines I set for myself. You all are my happiness. You keep me going and keep me shining every single day. You're the reason I laugh and love so hard.

Thank you to Ari, Willow, Lark, Cora, and Mads for being my safe space. For lifting me up when everything gets hard and I don't think I'm going to make it. You all make me smile every day, and I'm forever grateful to my small, beautiful circle.

Thank you so much to Dena. Gah, your kindness and love is another bright light in my life. You aren't just my editor—though please never leave me—you're my friend, and I'm so grateful to you. Writers who need an editor, no one will ever take as good of care of you as Dena Mastrogiovanni. I cannot recommend her more. She's fabulous.

And to all my readers, I never thought I'd have this life. I never thought when I was a young girl, lying in bed and wondering what my life would be like, that I'd get a chance to do what I love every single day. That I could write these stories in my head and people would want to read them.

I am so thankful to you all for reading these stories and for loving them. I love each and every one of you, and I want you to go for your dreams too. I want you to find that happiness and hold onto it.

Love you all!

—Nicole

FOLLOW ME

Facebook
  Instagram
  Amazon
  Goodreads
  Bookbub
  Patreon
  Ream
  Newsletter
  Facebook Group

ALL BOOKS

STANDALONES

Immoral (Rockstar/ Sports)
https://amzn.to/3x7HGfJ
Totally Schooled (Single Father/ Kindergarten Teacher)
https://amzn.to/3NTrwfC
Backslide (Second Chance)
https://amzn.to/3LDVIte
Hostile (High School Grumpy/Sunshine)
https://amzn.to/3JgjaLA
Outcast (Friends to Lovers)
https://amzn.to/3BvRGBf
Unfortunate (Island/First Love)
https://tinyurl.com/4z3pz5u9

ON THE TRACK SERIES

The Pretty Boy vs The Bad Boy
http://tinyurl.com/4sk3h4em
The Hotshot vs The Reporter
http://tinyurl.com/bbejs8sv
The Pro vs The Fan
http://tinyurl.com/ydc92p2r
The Rookie vs The Ace
http://tinyurl.com/3tcjk4nu

SPARK OF HOPE SERIES

Bruised But Not Broken (Friends to Lovers set around a trauma support group)
https://amzn.to/3Nfu6fn
Stalked But Not Afraid (Cop/camboy set around a trauma support group)
https://amzn.to/3xcstsW
Wrecked But Not Ruined (Friends to Lovers set around a trauma support group)
https://amzn.to/42BtFnV
Abandoned But Not Alone (Single Parent/ friends to lovers set around a trauma support group)
https://amzn.to/3JAB6mC
Crushed But No Defeated (Enemies to lovers set around a trauma support group)
https://amzn.to/3JPOu7r

KENSLEY PANTHERS SERIES

Keeper (Small town/High School/Friends to Lovers)
https://amzn.to/3MYz8gT
Guarded (Small town/Frenemies to lovers)
https://amzn.to/3yODiSj
Defender (Small Town/Frenemies to Lovers)
https://amzn.to/3FAGUuT

Rivaled (Small Town)
https://amzn.to/3n5MZJC
Protector (Small Town/Friends to Lovers)
https://amzn.to/3LyuzeA

CO-WRITES WITH CORA ROSE

Reaching Reed (Camboys/Friends to Lovers)
https://amzn.to/3yNgbaM
Becoming Bennet (Camboys/Frenemies to Lovers)
http://tinyurl.com/mtmf445s
Discovering Damon (Friends to lovers/Camboys)
http://tinyurl.com/mvs2s7hx
Sunshine For Sale
http://tinyurl.com/y98cppn2

KEEPER

Want some small town high school goodness? Don't forget to check out my Kensley Panthers Series! Starting with Keeper!
https://amzn.to/3MYz8gT

KEEPER

CAMDEN

"**C**ome on, Wells," I shout as the football spirals through the night sky toward my best friend. Players clash everywhere on the field, and the crowd is loud as hell, but all I see is Kingston Wells. My best friend, the team's tight end and number thirty-two out on the field.

When he catches it, he doesn't hesitate. He runs. He's fast, incredibly fast. And no one can catch him. I know it. He knows it. The crowd knows it as they chant his last name, and he runs it in for the final touchdown, just in time to claim the win.

Garrison Dixon, number twenty-four, wastes no time hoisting me up in the air to celebrate our big win, shouting over the crowd while I tap on his helmet, telling the big dummy to put me down. But he doesn't.

We're all on a high.

I see Kingston running toward us, his red helmet in hand. When he shoves Dixon playfully, that's when my feet finally touch the field below. Then Kingston's bigass arms are wrapped around me as we all jump up and down, surrounded by the rest of the school, who've rushed the football field to congratulate us.

Hell, the entire damn town is around us, chanting our names and our school. Taunting the other team who just lost, because they're our biggest rivals. *The Big Bend Bears. Eat it, suckers. We won this round.*

"We're the Kensley Panthers. Mighty, mighty, panthers," the cheer-leaders chant, loud and proud. In western Kansas—literally in the middle of nowhere—this is what we do on Friday nights.

The whole town shuts down until after the game, and then we party. It's all there is to do in this town of nine hundred people. And maybe some days, I can barely stand it, but nights like tonight, I ride the high and bask in the cheers of the crowd. Watching the smile on my best friend's face, I try my best to enjoy it. To let go of all my responsibilities, if only for the moment.

Kingston says this is the best time of our lives. *Me? I'm not so sure about that.* I don't want to really believe that, but as I look around at the middle-aged men wearing their old high-school football rings— some of them state championship rings—I think maybe he could be right. Because they're all stuck in that time.

Will that be Kingston and me someday?

Maybe.

And while that's a comforting thought to Kingston, it's a terrifying one for me.

This can't be all we are.

We all shower and change after the game. Kingston and I are the last to head out of the locker-room. His arm drapes over my shoulder. "Hell of a game, QB."

I roll my eyes, but I can't hold back the smile on my face. "Don't call me that. We've known each other since we were four. It's weird."

"Aw, you'll always be my quarterback though." I roll my eyes again, but he only chuckles, a happy laugh falling from his lips. "Fine, *Prescott*. Where are we celebrating tonight?"

I guess using my last name is better than fucking QB. I don't want to *just* be the high-school quarterback. I never have. But appar-ently, the one thing my deadbeat dad gave me before disappearing right after my seventh birthday was one hell of a throwing arm. "I can't. Mom picked up an extra shift at the tavern. I gotta watch Lucy."

My mom had Lucy almost five years ago, when I was thirteen. And even though we don't share the same dad, that kid means everything to me. Blonde hair and blue eyes, she must have gotten from her dad because my mom and I both have brown hair and green eyes. But Lucy is the happiest kid ever.

Don't know where she got that either.

Kingston seems to be thinking that over for a moment—thinking too hard, if you ask me—and he shrugs. "Okay. Sounds good. Let's go party with little Lucy. I'm here for it. That kid is funny as hell."

I shove him off me, pulling the keys to my beat-up old truck out of my jeans pocket. "You don't need to hang out with a four-year-old after we just won that game. She's probably already in bed, anyway. Go party. Tell me about it tomorrow, and don't do anything stupid."

"First of all, she's almost five. She wants a princess party, by the way." He grabs his own keys, heading for his obnoxious early 70's Mustang that's parked next to my truck. "Second, I miss Luce. I gotta go say hi. I am her favorite, after all."

Isn't that the truth?

I don't know why my sister is so in love with him—okay, maybe that's a lie—but it still stings when I'm usually the one taking care of her when we aren't in school. Mom works a lot to make up for being a single mom, and I don't mind picking up the slack. Like I said, Lucy is a cool kid. *It's fine. It's completely fine.*

"Kennedy is going to be pissed off if you don't party with her tonight." I say, pulling open the heavy door to my truck.

He waves that off like I knew he would. "Nah. She's probably already halfway through a bottle of Jack. She'll be fine."

My brow furrows, looking at him over the top of my truck. "You don't care that your girlfriend is getting drunk around a bunch of horny football players on a high from a win, and probably other shit?"

He runs his hand through his still-damp dark-brown hair and just laughs like he always does. His blue eyes sparkle with laughter because Kingston Wells is a happy guy—he can't help it. Nothing is really serious to Kingston. "She's a big girl. She can take care of herself."

He's not wrong. Kennedy Reeves is head cheerleader, blond, gorgeous, and the girl who punched Oakley Easton in seventh grade for grabbing her ass when we were all playing around out at the lake. She's a badass, all right. She's been Kingston Wells's girlfriend for two years now. They're the *It* couple in school. And she's one of my best friends too. "Yeah, no doubt. Though, it should still probably bug you."

"Let's go." He doesn't spend any more time talking about it, and instead of arguing with him like I probably should, we drive to my house to send my mom off to work and watch Lucy.

Like I assumed, Lucy's already in bed. Mom gave her a snack and a drink of water before tucking her in, so she'll probably be out for the night. Mom gives Kingston and me each a kiss on the cheek before rushing out, and we hang out on the couch, eating popcorn and absently watching whatever is on TV while reliving the game, play-by-play.

This is my typical Friday night.
And honestly, I wouldn't change it.
Not yet, anyway.

IMMORAL

How about a rockstar and professional baseball player romance? I have you covered!

https://amzn.to/3x7HGfJ

IMMORAL

PROLOGUE

"What are you doing over here by yourself, loser?"

Grady fucking Bell.

I smile at the sound of my best friend's voice coming from behind me while I sit on the dock, staring at the rippling water in the moonlight. I'm holding onto the neck of a whiskey bottle resting between my legs, but I haven't had much to drink tonight. It's graduation night. I should be happy. I *am* happy.

My dreams are about to come true. So are his.

But those dreams are sending us in completely different directions.

I feel his body crowd mine as he takes a seat on the end of the dock with me, his sneakers dangling just above the water like my own. "There's an epic party going on right back there." He extends his lanky arm behind us, that bigass grin with his bright, white teeth visible in the night.

"Aren't you tired of partying yet, Grady?"

He laughs at that, effortless and contagious. Grady is larger than life. He was even when we were in second grade, never caring what anyone thought about him. He can hit a home run effortlessly. Get an A on a test without even studying. Sing any song in existence acapella while bringing the biggest badass out there to tears. Score the winning touchdown in the last few seconds of a game. Play a song on his guitar perfectly after only hearing it once.

Grady Bell is a goddamn legend in this town, and now he's leaving.

"We're just getting started, Bailey."

I roll my eyes at the use of my last name but still smile because it's something he's always done. *Bell and Bailey.* In a small town like ours, that meant we were always paired together. School. Sports. Newspaper achievements.

Always.

"Seems to me, *Bell*, that we *were* just getting started, but then you had to go and sign with a record label."

He gives me a sly grin and steals the whiskey bottle from between my thighs, even though I can smell the booze on him already. "You want me to tell them to fuck off?" I turn to look at him and that intoxicating grin on his face. "Because I fucking will."

I laugh and look out at the lake water again. We both had baseball scholarships to the same college. That was the plan. It's always been my plan, decided for me before I was even born by a father with the same dream for himself.

Unfortunately, my mom got pregnant in an "oops" situation during their senior year of high school, and my dad proposed, then immediately went to trade school to learn to be a welder. I think it was then he decided I would be the baseball player.

And I'm not half bad.

Grady, the talented motherfucker, is good at all he does and, of course, excelled at baseball along with everything else. So, we decided that was our ticket out of this town. The major leagues. We'd play for the big boys, party like crazy, buy our moms houses, and never come back to this small town.

But instead, he had to go and get signed with a record label who wants him to immediately go to LA and lay tracks for an album. I'm happy for him. Music has always been his favorite talent, but I'm a selfish asshole, feeling lost and abandoned.

"No." I turn to look at Grady, his black hair just a little overgrown and blowing in the wind, and even though I can't see his dark green eyes, I know they're sparkling with mischief. "I want you to go and blow their fucking minds."

His grin widens. "You know I will. And you?"

I shrug and swallow hard, still facing him. "Me?"

"You're going to kill it in college sports, and then you're going to the MLB. You're going to the big leagues, and they won't even know what hit them."

How can I do that without Grady?

What's a catcher without his pitcher?

I don't recognize my own voice as I shift my body so I'm facing him directly, pulling my legs up on the dock and tucking them under me awkwardly. "What if I fail?"

He places the whiskey bottle next to him and then turns his body, mimicking my position. His large hands grip my face, not letting me look away. "Ryan, when have you ever failed in your life?"

When hasn't he been there to back me up? It's what I want to ask, but I don't. I just shake my head, taking his hands with me as I do. "I'm scared."

I hate making this admission. Men don't get scared. And if we do, we sure as hell don't admit it. In a small town like this in Kansas, men are still supposed to be "tough." We don't show weakness. "Me too."

I'm shocked when he readily admits this. Grady isn't afraid of anything. "You'll be fine."

"I'm going to California, Ry. This is all I've ever known." He doesn't release me, but he looks around the lake. No one is around us, but I hear the music coming from the shabby cabin our class rented for the weekend, and I can see the bonfire they've lit close to it.

"You'll be great."

His eyes meet mine, and I feel that familiar feeling stirring low in my belly. One I've been trying to ignore for years. One I've tried to drink away. I've tried my best to get lost in the girls in our class and out on the baseball field. I've thrown myself into everything else, trying like hell to ignore the one thing I know deep down I want.

Him.

"So will you."

"Chances of going pro are slim," I say lamely, my eyes transfixed on his full lips. No wonder he has such a reputation for being a good kisser. With lips like those, how could he not be?

Of course, that's only with girls.

Every fucking girl in our school.

Grady is, no doubt, straight. And I . . . I have no idea what I am.

Lost.

That seems about right.

He cups the back of my neck with one of his hands and pulls me close, resting his forehead against mine in a gesture he's done a lot when I've doubted myself. "Not for you. You're Ryan fucking Bailey. You're going to go far. You were destined for this."

A shiver runs through me from the intensity of his eyes on mine. "You're always so sure."

"About you? Of course, I am."

I want to lean in even closer. I breathe him in and hope like hell it's not noticeable, but I can't resist. He smells like whiskey and the lake from swimming earlier. And him. Just fucking him.

"Grady?" My voice is full of gravel as he pulls back enough to look into my eyes. His breathing seems rapid, but maybe it's my imagination.

"Yeah?"

I swear his gaze drops to my lips, but I try to shake that thought away. I've wanted him for years, but there's no way he feels the same. "I don't know what I was going to say," I admit.

"You think too much, Bailey. You always have." His thumb on his free hand—the other is still cupping the back of my neck—runs over my bottom lip, and I think I stopped breathing.

When he leans closer to me, I'm almost certain I'm dreaming. Or maybe I fell into the lake and am drowning. *Hell, maybe I'm dead.*

But when his firm lips press against mine, I couldn't give a fuck if I'm actually dead because this is my heaven.

His hand around the back of my neck grips me tighter and pulls me closer as a growl escapes my throat, and I don't think . . . I just attack his mouth with mine. Taking everything I've wanted for so damn long.

My hands move to his thick, soft hair, threading my fingers through it and pulling him to me, not able to get close enough. His mouth opens for me as my tongue darts inside, tasting Grady. *Finally.*

God, he tastes good.

Our moans mingle as he shoves me onto my back on the dock, and I think this is it. This is when he'll wake up from his drunken daze and punch me right in the face.

But he doesn't.

Instead, his body covers mine, settling between my legs, and I know he can feel how hard I am. But what really fucking shocks me to my core, something I'll never forget for as long as I live, is the erection that's *not* mine. His hard dick is pressed against mine as our lips meet again, and we grind against each other. Groaning and moaning with need as we kiss and writhe on the old wooden dock. My body is larger than his—both in pure muscle mass and in height—but he has no problem taking control, grabbing both my hands and pinning them above my head as our clothed cocks rub against each other, and I'm about to lose my mind.

"Grady," I gasp, close to coming in my jeans.

He pulls back enough to look down into my eyes, not releasing his hold on me. "Yeah?"

"What are we doing?"

I could kick myself for stopping this, but this is Grady. He doesn't make out with guys. *I can't be a drunken mistake. Not to him.*

"Celebrating?" His right eyebrow kicks up along with a cocky grin spreading on his too handsome face.

I'm shocked he isn't flipping the fuck out. But again, this is Grady. He doesn't freak out. He's calm, cool, and collected. Always. It's why he's a fucking fantastic pitcher. Nothing rattles him. "Like this?" I rasp as I feel his body on top of mine while I pant and plead with him silently to come back to me.

The spell broken, he sits up, letting go of my wrists and kneeling between my legs. "Maybe not the best idea."

It's like a knife plunging into my heart, but deep down I know he's right. There are so many things I want to say to him. I want to pull him back to me, kiss the fuck out of him, and tell him I'm an idiot for saying anything. To get lost with me.

But I don't. Instead, I take his hand when he stands and then pulls me up, ruffling my hair in the casual, easy way that's just Grady.

He isn't freaking out that he kissed a guy. His thoughts aren't swirling around in his head that's moving far away while I'm staying in the same state where we grew up. He doesn't worry about any of that.

"Come on, fucker. This is our last night before the real world comes calling and we make it our bitch."

I follow, but it's on shaky, uncertain legs.

Because now, I've had a fucking taste. And I have no idea how I'm going to come back from that.

Made in United States
North Haven, CT
08 November 2024

60024505R00117